a30118 037345737b

THE COUNTRY ONES

THE
COUNTRY
ONES

Mary Curran

Illustrated by
Elizabeth Trimby

1975
CHATTO & WINDUS
LONDON

Published by
Chatto & Windus Ltd.
42 William IV Street
London WC2N 4DF

*

Clarke, Irwin & Co. Ltd.
Toronto

17523245

03734573

ISBN 0 7011 2085 1

© Mary Curran 1975

Printed in Great Britain by
T. and A. Constable Ltd.
Hopetoun Street, Edinburgh

Contents

Chapter One

AGGIE stood at the door listening for Ma coming down the lane from the morning milking. She had just finished knotting the red ribbons into her two long plaits of hair, and was watching the two cats sitting crouched on a sunny patch of earth. They would be the first to hear the scuff of Ma's clogs and then the hens would come running and squacking and Henry, the pig, would grunt and squeal from his sty at the end of the garden, for everybody needed Ma to get their breakfast. Aggie had done her share. The kettle was boiling at the side of a good red fire on the kitchen range and her two young sisters, Katy and Janey, were both awake. She could hear the squeals and scuffles of them both, carrying on in the big bed where the three of them slept.

She stept out into the sunshine, her feet dragging a bit in the new black leather school boots. They felt like a ton weight after a summer spent mostly in her bare feet. The rough roads would soon wear down the tackets, Da had said. It would take months, Aggie knew.

The morning sun was shining on the light mists that lay on the fields and everything glimmered and glistened right away to the far orchard at the side of the river. The river was quiet today because the water was low and it flowed silently over the shifting sands. A thick belt of reeds grew along its edges and you could see the sloe bushes and haw-thorns and queen-of-the-meadow nodding along the tops of its high clay banks.

Aggie shuddered at the thought of the curving river and its flat full look of clay-coloured water when the tide came creeping up from the bay. She was afraid of its stillness and soughing reeds and she would never forget about the two boys who were picking hawthorn blossoms and stepped into the quicksands. The only trace of them was the branches of blossom sticking up out of the ooze.

'Aggie, is there something to see?' Janey, in bare feet and long flannelette nightgown, called out from the doorway.

'No. There's nothing,' she shrugged. 'And you'd better get your clothes on, you and Katy. Ma's coming!' She followed the cats into the lane, still looking down at the boots, thinking that they looked twice as big as last year; and there was Ma arriving with the can of new milk.

Aggie suddenly smiled. Of all the people in the world she liked Ma the best with Da alongside of that. Ma would never know this nor Da either, for folk in the Lowlands were not given to showing their feelings.

'It's gan to be anither fine harvest day, Agnes,' Ma said, the warm smell of the cows still about her. 'And a good day for the start of the school!'

Aggie took her mother's arm.

'It's still just after seven, Ma. There's plenty of time!'

'Ye've had a fine lang holiday,' Ma smiled. 'More than six weeks running wild and not learning a thing!'

Aggie followed her mother into the house without answer-ing for she knew what Ma thought about learning, although she did not always agree. Then she went to help Janey, who was only six, with her clothes and hair while Ma set the frying pan on the hob for the breakfast.

'I was hoping it would rain!' the ten-year-old Katy was

8

complaining. 'You don't feel so bad when it rains on the first day of the school. Just look at these long black stockings and big heavy boots! Heel shods, toe shods, studs and tackets! And the town ones will still be in sand-shoes!'

'Well, we have them on Sunday,' said Janey.

'I'm talking about today!' argued Katy, pushing her fair hair from the front of her eyes. 'And you've got your frock on the wrong way round!'

'So you have!' said Aggie. 'Stand still, Janey, and I'll change it.'

'Some frocks have buttons down the front,' trembled Janey. 'I've seen them in the catalogue. I thought everybody would think it was a new frock and not Katy's from last year.'

'Nobody will notice it was Katy's!' Aggie soothed her. 'She's got mine on. Ma buys us all the same kind so nobody can tell.'

'When I'm big,' Katy announced firmly, 'I'm having nothing but high-heeled shoes with pointed toes like hen's nebs!'

She stamped noisily with the heavy boots on the tile floor.

'I like my bare feet the best,' said her young sister. 'Oh Aggie, you're pulling my hair!'

'I'm just tying the ribbons. There, go and wash your face!'

One by one they were ready and clattered up the lobby to the kitchen where Ma was bending over something sizzling on the range.

'Do we have a whole egg, Ma?' Janey asked.

'Oh, I think so. The hens are laying well enough,' Ma replied, looking round and surveying them with satisfaction. 'Sit in at the table. You look nice and tidy, I'm sure. Agnes, take care of your skirt. It will have to do for Sundays and all till you get a new one and that's not before the pig's slaughtered!'

'The boots are too heavy, Ma,' Katy grumbled.

'Now then, Katy, no complaining!' Ma warned her. 'The days are not always fine like this one. It's nearly the end of August and a long winter lies ahead. Besides,' her lined face broke into a warm smile, 'anybody that sees your nice clean face and fine head of hair, will never notice your boots!'

'They'll just hear them, Ma!' Katy giggled, regaining her good humour for her moods changed very quickly. 'They'll think it's Baron's Pride!' and she pointed to the photo of the stallion above the mantelpiece with the portraits of Granda and Grandma Breen on one side and Grandma and Grandfather Kenny on the other.

Aggie took a quick look at herself in the little mirror hung above the enamel wash-basin. She was tall and thin for her age and could see into the mirror well enough although Ma warned her plenty against vanity. She had a small freckled face with blue eyes and her long fair hair, like her sisters, had a shining yellow tinge and was Ma's greatest pride. Aggie knew that on the fine Sundays when they went to church with their hair hanging loose to their waists, the greatest compliment that Ma could get, was for someone to say 'My, Mrs Kenny, the girls' hair does you credit! But it must be a lot of work!'

Then Ma would give her nervous little cough and answer, 'Oh, indeed, it's no work at all!'

'And you never think of getting their hair bobbed?'

Ma's voice was raised in horrified protest.

'Goodness no! Bobbed hair just makes a girl look like a boy! And that's not right!'

So Aggie knew that she and Katy and Janey would be wearing plaits for many a day yet, and would have to put up with Ma's fierce fine-toothed combings and head-washings which always followed when a hand was raised to explore the least tickle among the hair.

'Now then, Agnes, come on, like a good lass! Standin' there dreamin'! I have to get on with the work. Your Auntie Lizzie will be out today!'

'Oh, so she is!' Aggie quickly came back into the kitchen. 'And we'll miss her too, unless she stays till night time!'

'She always stays till night time!' said Katy. 'How else could Jamie Watson meet her up the road?'

'Now then, Katy, don't let me hear you at that talk again!' Ma said crossly. 'We've all kent Jamie Watson for years anyway!'

'But Ma, everybody's always asking us when Auntie Lizzie and Jamie are getting married! Aren't they, Aggie?' Katy turned to her sister.

'Even the ones at the school!' Janey put in.

'And, Ma, we don't know what to say because all the folks know that Granda will not have Auntie Lizzie marry Jamie Watson, because he's not christened,' Katy explained seriously. 'And what for is he not christened?'

'Jamie's father just didn't believe in christening,' Ma answered as she buttered scones at the end of the table. 'Agnes, how many scones can you eat for your dinner piece?'

'Two,' said Aggie promptly. 'Treacle.'

'But, Ma . . .' Katy began again.

'Wheesht now, Katy. That will do,' Ma told her. 'Your grandfather knows best.'

'Did Da leave us a penny, Ma?' Aggie asked.

'Aye, he did. There's three at the corner of the mantel-piece.'

'Hurray! I think I'll buy a new pencil!'

'A pencil!' cried Janey in disgust. 'A bar of toffee is more like it. I'll bring you back some, Ma!'

'That'll be nice, Janey!' Ma patted her youngest on the cheek. 'And be sure and do what Mrs McMinn tells you! And you too Katy! And this is the year you have the Qualifying examination, Agnes. Next April, isn't it?'

Aggie had a sudden leaden feeling in her chest and her appetite disappeared. The Qualifying! So it was. That had been the teacher's doing. That had been Mrs McMinn who had talked Ma and Da into that.

'It's a fine new scheme in education. It gives the chance of going to the High School to boys and girls whose folk would find it too big a strain to pay for their books and fees, Mrs Kenny,' Mrs McMinn, the teacher, had explained when she came out one day during the summer holidays. 'It costs such a lot nowadays to bring up a family that all sorts of people are taking advantage of it for their children. And of course, the size of the bursary varies with the means of the family.'

Ma was carried away, for this was the answer to a prayer that had lain deep within her ever since Aggie started the school.

'I've always wondered what I could get for the lassies that would better them,' she confided humbly to Mrs McMinn. 'But is Agnes clever enough to pass this—this Qualifying?'

'Clever!' The teacher snorted and the bunch of coloured feathers in her hat shook furiously. 'It's a matter of working hard enough and,' she added with great tact, 'I've no doubt she'll get a full bursary should she be successful!'

So Aggie found herself among the three candidates of the Qualifying Class in Mrs McMinn's little school.

For a moment she wished she was her brother John who had left school in the summer or Robert who was already sixteen. Just then they were likely among the stooks in the harvest field along with Da, far from Mrs McMinn's sharp tongue and cane.

'There's nothing like learnin',' Ma was saying as she put the 'pieces' into the separate schoolbags along with the yellow oilskins and sou'westers which they always carried. 'Your father or me never had such a chance. We were both working at thirteen and your brothers had to leave at fourteen to earn their keep. So see that you lassies stick in! I don't want to see you work as hard as I've had to do. Five in the morning is too early a start. Are you listening, Agnes?'

'Yes, Ma!' Aggie nodded and her eyes filled with sudden tears.

She knew fine what Ma meant, for as well as Da, there was five of a family, some hens, a pig, and milking to do up at the Farm morning and night. Ma had little time to herself and no money to waste, although times had not been just as hard since the boys had started to work. This summer Aggie had worked too, in the turnip field for about three weeks of the holidays, along with a squad of other children from the town and the Hill Village. She had earned enough to help buy her boots and oilskins, for there was a walk to the school of almost three miles and the weather and roads in winter were rough and wet. Ma believed in proper clothes for bad weather, for illness meant having the Doctor and he had to be paid. Everybody living in the Little Valley and the Hill Village and in the Glen beyond, thought there was nobody like the Doctor, but for all that, where there was not much money they all had to stay healthy.

Aggie blinked the tears away before anybody saw them for Katy's eyes were as sharp as a hawk's.

'I'll try hard, Ma,' she said, getting up from the table. 'I think I'll go and see Henry before I leave for the school.'

Henry was the pig, and he had come by that name because one of the pigs reigning in the sty long before him had been bought from a man called Henry, and the name stuck to each one in turn. Henry's sty was at the bottom of the vegetable garden behind the house. The girls made a pet of him and when they called his name, he squealed with excitement, and stood up on his hind-legs and leaned his forepaws and big, hairy pink head on the front ledge. When he got too fat and heavy to manage this, they knew that his days were numbered. This usually happened in the back end of the year, and the three girls sorrowed for days, although the money was used to buy the things they all needed. Then a new little pig appeared in the sty to be fattened up too, and they fell in love with him all over again.

The sun was warm outside and the air smelled of corn sheaves heavy with dew and wet leaves that were ripe but not yet ready to fall.

A light haze lay on the hills in the east and Cairnsmore-of-Fleet, the colour of lavender, was a faint outline.

'There's no cap of cloud on the big hill today!' Aggie

13

said to herself. 'He raised it to the sun early this morning, very likely!' for it was well known that Cairnsmore only raised his cap to two people—the sun and the wind.

From Andrew Blackwell's farm up the lane came the rumble of carts, and the sound of men's voices. Aggie stood still and listened on the step of the pig-sty. Da's voice would be among them, but it could never be heard from here, as he always spoke so quietly. He spoke to his horses too, in the same tone he used to people. 'Now then, Trimmie Lass, a wee bit further!' he would coax the little mare, but his voice took on a sterner edge when Charlie, the big Clydesdale, was showing off.

'Behave yourself, sir! That's just enough! Don't have me tell you again!'

For a silent moment he would stare severely at the big horse, as though he were scolding one of his children, and Charlie would toss his great head and then drop it in obedience.

Everybody knew that Da had a way with horses. They nickered and whinnied when they heard his voice, and when it was his turn to go to church on Sunday and Ma's to stay at home, they followed him up the hedgeside as far as they could go and then waited to escort him back again on his way home.

'Come on, Aggie! We're ready!' Katy's voice rang out 'You weren't so fond of Henry yesterday!'

'Coming,' Aggie answered, and with a 'Ta ta, Henry,' to the pig, who grunted in reply, she raced back to the front of the house.

'If you buy a pencil, I'll buy a rubber!' Katy suggested, as she slung her schoolbag over her shoulder. 'Then we'll halve them and have a bit each!'

'Yes, we'll do that,' Aggie agreed, wishing she had such clever ideas. Her mind always seemed to be tangled up with birds' nests or coloured leaves or the clouds in the sky, never with the sensible things that tumbled out of Katy without any trouble.

Ma stood in the doorway with her hands below her apron, giving her usual schoolday warning.

'Be good lassies, now! And don't be talking to folk you don't know! You never can tell who's on the road these days.'

Putting her arm round the three of them she walked on to the middle of the lane. 'You're in nice time. Maybe you'll see Da and the boys in the harvest field. That big field between the sauch trees and the Gow Burn has to be cut out yet. Look after your young sister, Agnes!'

'So I will, Ma!'

'Come straight home at night. Ta-ta!'

'Ta-ta, Ma!' they all called out, and Aggie added: 'I'll gather blackberries from the fieldsides when I come home. Ta ta!'

They set off up the lane, turning round to wave to Ma now and again until they reached the Rosy Hollow where the road dipped and curved and Ma was no longer in view.

'I wish it was the summer holidays just starting!' Katy gulped.

'It's not that long since we got our holidays, is it, Aggie?' Janey asked from behind, where she always walked. 'Maybe the school only starts next week!'

'There is no fear of that!' sighed Aggie. 'Mrs McMinn told us on Sunday at the church. Can you not walk just a wee bit quicker, Janey?'

'I'm coming, Aggie, as quick as I can!'

'She's out of the habit because of the holidays,' Katy said.

'That's it!' cried Janey. 'I'll walk quicker the next day. Aggie, what's christened?'

'Six years of age and doesn't know what christened is,' scoffed Katy. 'It's easy to be christened. You get water poured on you!'

'Oh!'

'Everybody got christened when they were born except Jamie Watson and his father wouldn't have it,' explained Aggie.

'If Jamie gets christened then he can marry Auntie Lizzie. Granda Breen has given his word,' Katy said.

'Maybe we would be asked to the spree!' mused Aggie. 'There's cake and dancing at a marriage, and Katy, you could sing "Oh, Rowan Tree!".'

They were now just approaching the Farm where they waved to Miss Blackwell, the farmer's sister and they saw Da and the boys in one of the far away cornfields. After that there were no houses until they reached the town.

Round the little bend just beyond the Farm the lane stretched emptily ahead until it joined the Big Road.

Aggie liked the empty road. She felt safer when she saw no people. On one side the high thorn hedge rustled and nodded lazily in the light wind, showing here and there the bright gleam of blackberries and the scarlet of rose-hips. On the other side was the stone dyke almost covered with whins and with red campions and harebells growing in the rough roadside grass. The pattern was broken only by the Little Wood which now was dark and secret under the heavy full leaf of late summer.

It was a country world that made up the Little Valley hemmed in between Barr in the west and Larg in the east, with Cairnsmore looming behind for the sun to climb over in the morning. The town and the higher hills lay to the north and the river curved and twisted its way southward through the valley into the bay about eight miles away.

Aggie had been at the other side of the Barrhill when she went to visit Grandma and Grandfather Kenny who lived in a little town near the sea. But of the world beyond the long blue hump of Cairnsmore she knew little, except that the main railway line from the town disappeared behind it and went as far as London, 380 miles away. This distance was correct as everybody knew for so it was written on the milestone which leaned against the Big Wall just outside the town.

Every night, except Sunday night, an express train to London rumbled down the line like a big glow-worm, uttered a shriek, sometimes despairing and lonely, sometin ˙s merry, and gay, as it crossed the iron bridge which spa ned the river, and then dwindled away into the dark. In he early morning another train from London chugged its way up the line, but Aggie very seldom heard it for she was in her deep sleep, and anyway, the coming back from an adventure could never be the same as the start of it.

Lying in her bed, many a night Aggie wondered what it would be like to arrive in a city or a big town and she could only imagine streets packed with people like it was on the Cattle Show day in the county town.

They were just leaving the lane and had reached the main road when Janey said her legs were tired and Aggie realized she had been walking too fast.

'I'll take your bag, Janey!' she said, stopping for a moment. 'We're in plenty of time. There's the milk lorry at Tom Kie's!' and she slung Janey's schoolbag over her other shoulder.

'Sometimes when I look quick at my boots, I think they're not that big!' Katy said, looking down at her feet. 'And sometimes I think they're just like Wallie Johnstone's!'

They all giggled. The length of Wallie's feet was well known and the lightness of them too, for if ever there was a poacher, he was one.

'I'm hoping the stour hides the size of mine,' Aggie answered. 'I'm a size bigger than last year!'

'I've heard Miss Blackwell and Ma say in the byre sometimes that Wallie would like Auntie Lizzie too!' Katy announced as they started off again.

'I've heard that often before! And he needn't bother,' replied Aggie. 'For Jamie has courted Auntie Lizzie since she was sixteen. And he never forgot her even when he was away at the Great War! Mind you, Wallie has nice black hair!'

'It's not nearly as nice as Hughie Grant's, the milk-tester's!' Katy said to that. 'His hair is all nice wee waves, that curl up at the end!'

'Oh, I never noticed it!'

They lapsed into silence again as they crossed the Big Road to the sidewalk. It was a wide tarred road and Aggie liked the smell of it when the summer sun brought the tar bubbling up into smooth blisters. Running along the pavement side was a high stone wall that enclosed a private estate. It was too smooth for climbing and therefore the other side had all the flavour of a mystery, although they knew that cattle grazed there in the well-kept green fields.

Although it was still early in the day, a few motor-cars and vans were passing along the road. Aggie always looked at them with great curiosity for Da said that they were a menace to folk and that they went far too fast and frightened the horses.

'Young Dan Griffin has a new motor!' Katy said. 'John told me.'

'Maybe so,' retorted Aggie, 'but old Donald, his father, still has the pony.'

'Tom Hannah, the grocer, says he'll have a motor-van for the incoming year!' argued Katy, who liked all this progress.

Aggie sighed. Even the doctor had got a motor-car, although he still kept his horse, not like some of them.

After they had passed the Chestnut Wood and the milestone, the town, lying low on the banks of the river, came into sight, screened as always by a light cloud of smoky haze.

The heat of the sun had driven away the morning coolness and Aggie felt hot and sticky. Her heart began to sink for she did not like the town, and the arrow on the milestone pointing towards it depressed her further. The other arrow pointing in the opposite direction with 'London 380 miles' written above it, was a much more lighthearted one, for it also pointed the way home.

Aggie felt awkward and gawky next to the town girls. Their clothes were much lighter and shorter than her own, they wore shoes instead of boots and most of them seemed to pass the summer holidays picnicking on the river or visiting friends in big towns or even going to the seaside. At least Cathleen Gemmell and the McKay girls seemed to.

'I'm not going to say anything to any of them about working in the turnip field this summer,' she said to herself, 'and they'll likely ask.'

Now that the work was over, Aggie only remembered the best part of it. There had been about a score of children between ten and fourteen, crawling up the furrows with sacking round their knees, thinning the turnips and listening to Nathan Thomson whose job it was to look after the squad and keep them working, reciting poetry and verses of the Bible in his deep, rich voice.

The work was hard and the day long, and sometimes it was drizzling rain and yet not wet enough to shelter, or else it was very hot and turning to thunder and Nathan would try to keep the younger ones from becoming too frightened by reciting the Boston Burgular.

'Here comes the Boston burgular
With heavy chains he's bound. . .'

They listened with shaky smiles, one eye and one ear to the muttering heavens.

Everybody else knew that Nathan did not keep strictly to the truth and that his stories of France and the Dardanelles, and being torpedoed by a U-boat in the Atlantic, were other men's adventures and not his own, but when he leaned on his long hoe and said the Lord's Prayer, nobody uttered a word for it was so splendid.

He even knew what the people in France said. 'San Fairy Ann!' he told the children, 'that's what the folk in France always say, and I never found out what they were meaning!' With that he began to hoe out a few weeds while they all looked at him with sympathy.

'I hope that Mrs McMinn hasn't got a new cane!' Katy broke the silence. 'The old one was bad enough!'

'It's not the cane I'm worrying about,' answered Aggie, 'I've had it plenty of times anyway. It's that Qualifying!'

'If you go to the High School, Aggie,' Janey panted at

the back, 'will you speak to us? They say the High School girls are proud!'

'Pride is a deadly sin, Mrs McMinn says!' Katy warned them, and added mournfully, 'I'll be glad when we're on our way back home this night!'

The town straddled both sides of the river with an arched stone bridge connecting the two parts. On this side, the Old Village, where Grandma and Granda Breen lived, huddled low along its banks and across the bridge was the main shopping street, with the churches, schools, and big houses perched on the high ground above the town.

The road running through the Old Village was in line with the river and the main street of the town.

Mrs Gouldie's shop was just at the corner of the bridge where the village street began with the policeman's house and office just opposite and the public house close by. It was an old-fashioned little building and had been a toll house in the days when the river was forded where the bridge now stood.

She sold everything from paraffin to bootlaces and the shelves were a companionable mixture of semolina and pencils, jam and scrubbing-brushes, and her bars of toffee were longer for a penny than anybody else's.

'Get a bar of the green kind!' Katy urged Janey at the window. 'It's awfully big! Oh, there's the rubber I want!' and in she went.

'I wonder if Mrs Gouldie has had a dram!' Aggie said to Janey. 'I don't like her when she's like that!'

'I'll have the raspberry,' Janey mumbled, not listening to Aggie. 'I'll get your pencil when I'm in. A yellow or a red one?'

'A yellow one!' replied Aggie meekly, handing over her penny, and thinking herself a terrible fearty.

But then her sisters had not heard Mrs Gouldie that day in the summer, she thought, standing by herself outside the window. She would never forget that day. It was close, with heavy clouds, hanging black and ragged in the sky and not moving. Ma had run out of sugar, for she had been boiling up rhubarb into jam, and after using up all the crystallized, had had to turn to the household sugar, leaving herself short. Ma never liked to send Aggie on the road alone to the town, so she had let her wear her sandshoes so that she could hurry back.

The smell in Mrs Gouldie's shop was like New Year's Day and she herself was in fine fettle.

'It's the end of the world, I tell you!' she was roaring to the customer standing at the little counter. 'The end of the world is nigh.'

Aggie stood rooted in the doorway at the sound of these unexpected words of doom.

'I know it! Dae ye not see the darkenin' sky?'

Mrs Gouldie's fist came down with a heavy thud on the counter, for she was a big woman.

'There's the sign that the world is nearing its end! And there have been other signs too! First, the Great War, then the plague of Influenza—Agnes, what do you want standing there pantin'? Ye shouldn't run like that!'

'Two pounds of sugar, if you please!' Aggie managed to say.

'There ye are, then, and a sweetie forbye!' and Mrs Gouldie handed over the things with a grand gesture and a cloud of whisky breath.

'Thank you.' Aggie retreated quickly, her first thought to get home before the terrible prophecy was fulfilled.

She trotted along the dusty edge of the road, now and then daring to glance up at the lowering clouds, in case she might see some dreadful sign appearing out of the greyness.

She knew now that Mrs Gouldie had been 'at the bottle' as Da put it, but nevertheless she was glad when all three had left the shop and were crossing the bridge, munching a little piece of Janey's toffee.

'We'll give you a shot with the pencil and rubber when we get home, won't we, Aggie?' Katy promised grandly.

THE COUNTRY ONES

There were few people about and they were the only children as Mrs McMinn allowed the country ones to come in at half-past nine, instead of nine, owing to the distance they had to walk.

The town was a long street of granite houses and shops. Folk said it was a clean little town, ordinary in itself, but the view from the bridge when the river was still, and the houses and trees were reflected in the water, was something that visitors always admired.

But after heavy rain, or the melting snow came down from the hills, the river was swollen and the current flowed fast and dark. It tore along relentlessly under the bridge to the weir, where it broke up into a tumbling torrent of black water, edged with frothy cream. The deep silent flow was fascinating to look at over the parapet of the bridge when the moving river made you think you were moving too.

Nevertheless, it had always a fresh sparkle and ripple when it broke over the rocks on its path, for it had not yet acquired the stealth of the sandbanks and the reeds.

The school stood at the top of a steep hill and the three girls climbed it in silence.

'This time yesterday,' Aggie thought, 'I was running in the grass in my bare feet!'

At the school-gate they paused for a moment for from the open window came the buzz of children's voices and the loud, clear tones of Mrs McMinn.

'Bernard Jones, you great ninny, come out to the blackboard! To think that you have forgotten everything in such a short time! Tom Riley, you stay in your seat. I said Bernard Jones, and Bernard Jones it will be!' Then came the rattle of the cane banging on the teacher's desk and Aggie looked at her two sisters.

The church clock struck an ominous one. 'That's half past nine!' she whispered. 'We'd better go in!'

Tiptoeing into the porch, they hung up their coats and a few minutes later the teacher's voice greeted them as they entered the schoolroom.

THE COUNTRY ONES

'Come along, you Kenny girls! I'm waiting to say prayers and mark the register. Bernard Jones, get back to your seat. Agnes Kenny, as you are in the Qualifying Class along with Cathleen Gemmell and Helen McKay, take that desk in front of mine.'

'Yes, ma'am!' Aggie slid into her seat.

'Attention everyone!' The cane rattled on the desk and in complete silence Mrs McMinn opened the register and filled in the last of the names. Then she closed it, put it in a drawer and looked round at them all.

'Today is the start of another school year,' she said slowly and clearly. 'And I hope that each one of you will do your utmost to make it one of your best. It is also a very important year for you three girls who are in the Qualifying Class. If you are prepared to work hard enough to pass the Qualifying Examination, you will receive the advantages of a High School education. Such an education will not only improve your mind but will offer you better prospects for the future. It is not every child who gets this great opportunity.'

She looked steadily at the three of them and then went on in an even voice that was not usual for her.

'I want you to say a prayer, a special prayer, to your patron saint for help and guidance in your work, for your own sakes and for the good name of the school!'

Mrs McMinn's glance rested on Aggie and a little smile played at the corners of her mouth. For a fleeting moment the girl caught a glimpse of a warm, encouraging strength behind the worn, lined face of the teacher, and she felt ashamed of her unwillingness.

'Yes, ma'am,' she answered shyly.

'That's right, Agnes.' The teacher nodded slowly. 'That's right!' And then she called out in a loud voice to the school, 'Now all kneel and pray!'

Chapter Two

AGGIE had no liking for the first day of the school after the holidays, but it helped to be a future candidate for the Qualifying, as it gave her a certain importance.

The school had about thirty pupils from the five-year-old infants to the 'leavers' of fourteen, and Mrs McMinn was the only teacher. She had good eyesight, even in the back of her head, as they all knew, and Aggie imagined that she rarely took her eyes off her, and yet she managed to watch all the other pupils besides.

She was a great believer in the cane and Aggie saw that morning already many of the pupils holding out their right hands to receive one and sometimes two of Mrs McMinn's stinging whacks. On one occasion Katy was among the punished and Aggie, peering furtively at her sister's little freckled face and fair swinging plaits, felt a terrible resentment against the teacher, which she controlled very quickly. She knew the eagle eye of Mrs McMinn would pounce on her like a flash and a sharp rap over the knuckles would be her own reward.

To some of the bigger boys a slap with the cane was nothing, but in their case a lash of Mrs McMinn's tongue was added. Sometimes if anybody got a chance to glance out of the window overlooking the playground and the road, a row of passers-by would be seen leaning over the playground wall and listening with rapt attention to the clear flow of words that rolled from the teacher's lips out of the schoolroom window. This was especially the case on a Wednesday afternoon which was the town's half-holiday.

'You great lout of a boy! Some help you'll be to your parents when you're older, I'm sure. Some good you'll be to yourself, too! What do you think you're at school for? To work, boy, not to play! Stand up and hold out your hand!'

In spite of all this Mrs McMinn had a reputation for being a fine teacher and as her caning was no worse than that of the teachers in the other schools, the children quite liked her and certainly respected her. About once or twice a year she and Mr McMinn paid a visit to Aggie's mother and it always amazed the Kenny girls to hear her talk and laugh so merrily at their house.

'You would hardly think she was a teacher at all,' Aggie had remarked to Katy.

'That's because she's on her holidays as well,' Katy answered, and added: 'And, of course, she's wearing her Sunday hat with the feathers in it! It's bound to make a difference!'

Mr McMinn was a long-faced, melancholy man with a grey drooping moustache and red-rimmed watery eyes. He seldom spoke and never worked, but he kept house while Mrs McMinn was teaching.

Once someone visiting at Aggie's home had remarked that he had been a handsome well set-up man at one time. Aggie could hardly believe it. Many a time she tried to search Mr McMinn's face for a glimpse of his former glory, without success. And she had never yet seen his discontented mouth break into a smile.

Sometimes when the teacher was so minded, she would

25

have a reading session round her desk and she would talk of what the world was like when she was young, and the whole school would listen.

The Tay Bridge disaster gripped everybody's attention for it held first-hand information—'And this night it was wild and stormy and my father was standing at the door watching the train cross the bridge. Suddenly the lights seemed to do a strange dance and then they went out . . .'

She paused dramatically before she broke the tense silence with the rest of the story.

However, on the first day after the holidays Mrs McMinn was in no mood for telling stories. All she wanted was to get the school into its usual routine of learning as soon as possible in case the Inspector called, for she had, or pretended to have, a great fear of the Inspector.

The school was always pleased to see the Inspector, who was a big, rosy-faced man, pleasant and kindly. On his last visit he had, before seating himself, pulled up his trouser leg so far that a piece of bare white leg was revealed for anybody to see, above his rather short, black socks and boots. The fact that an Inspector possessed a bare leg like other people, had put the school entirely at its ease and everybody answered his questions so well that Mrs McMinn gave the pupils a half-holiday to celebrate their triumph.

Aggie, in spite of her good intentions, found it difficult to keep her mind on her work. Through the school windows she could see the sunlight shining on the roof of the row of little houses where Tom Riley's mother lived, and far, far beyond that was a line of blue and mauve hills. At home now, Ma would be putting the girdle on the fire and getting out the baking board to make her daily baking of scones.

'Maybe she'll make pancakes too, for Auntie Lizzie's visit.' Aggie was just considering when Mrs McMinn's cane suddenly descended smartly on her knuckles and the pancake vision fled.

'Agnes Kenny, if you think you're a born genius, then I don't!' the teacher's voice shrilled at her. 'If you want to pass examinations, you first have to work and not dream! Yes, work, and work hard!'

A slow flush crept over Aggie's neck and face and she felt that everybody had stopped working to look at her. 'Yes, ma'am,' she agreed hurriedly, rubbing the back of her hands.

'Then don't have me tell you again, Agnes!' Mrs Mc-Minn's tone was a little less stern. 'If you get through the High School, you'll certainly have good prospects later on! And just think what you'll be able to do for your parents and yourself!'

Aggie tackled the sums once again and the buzz of voices continued round her. There were the infants, the new-comers of that day, with a piece of soft clay in their hands, trying to model it into some recognizable object with their little untrained fingers. Janey's class was copying with pains-taking care the word 'penmanship' written on the black-board. This word was one of Mrs McMinn's favourite writing exercises. Other children were learning their arithmetic tables aloud and in the back row the older pupils were writing a composition with much thinking and rubbing out and a nudge and a whisper when they thought the teacher was giving her attention to some other unfortunate.

In the middle of the morning the bell on the teacher's desk was rung for a fifteen minute break and there was a scramble into the playground.

'Now then, girls first!' Mrs McMinn called out, trying to instil some chivalry into her pupils. 'Edward Campbell, do I see you pushing little Rose?'

'No, ma'am!' lied the boy cheerfully, as they marched out.

After the long holidays the three Kenny sisters felt a wide gap between themselves and the town children, who had been companions throughout the summer. For a little while they stood together in a corner of the playground eating one of their 'pieces'. Aggie broke off little bits of scone inside the paper bag and put them into her mouth for she did not like to eat in front of people. Very few of the town children brought a 'piece' and when they did they called it a sandwich, with the bread cut very thin.

Some of the children like Cathie Gemmell (who wore light sandals to Aggie's mortification) and the McKay sisters (in shoes!) were quite well dressed but others were poorly clad.

The Riley family, whose father had been killed in the Great War, were tidy and clean but Aggie had heard Ma say that Mrs Riley was nearly killing herself working to keep them fed and clothed. Sometimes Ma sent in eggs when the hens were laying well, along with an odd rabbit, for the laird had said Da could catch rabbits to feed his family, but not to sell, and Da reckoned that nobody would grudge one to the hungry Rileys.

Every time Aggie saw Mrs Riley she remembered her first year at the school. She had been sitting at her desk, trying to make pink paper roses, as Mrs McMinn had showed her, so that the middle stayed firm, when someone, making queer choking noises, came running through the playground and burst into the schoolroom. It was Mrs Riley sobbing wildly, and waving a piece of paper clutched in her hand.

Mrs McMinn had put her arm round her shoulder, and led her out, speaking to her in low tones until the terrible crying had subsided. She took her back through the playground on to the road and then the footsteps disappeared.

The school was stunned to silence.

'Mrs Riley has had word from the front!' somebody said at last. 'And the teacher is taking her home!' and they all looked at Tom Riley who was only seven and who began to cry.

Later on Mrs McMinn had included the soul of Private Riley in their prayers and for a long time after that many other names were mentioned of men who had once been boys in the town.

Eddie Campbell came and offered Aggie and her sisters some of his grandmother's home-made treacle toffee. He was a big boy who had no worries about heavy boots and warm clothing for his feet were bare and dirty, his elbows stuck out of his shirt and his trousers hung in ragged patches. Eddie, in his own words, had never had a father or mother; he just lived with his grandmother.

'Your grandmother makes good toffee!' Aggie said, chewing on a bit.

'Did you eat a piece of that toffee?' Cathie Gemmell came up and asked in a shocked voice. 'My mother says I'm not to take anything from some people! Come here!' and she whispered in Aggie's ear. 'The Campbells are not clean!'

Aggie looked at Eddie who was wrestling with a big lump of toffee in his mouth, his blue eyes glaring at Cathie from under a tow-coloured fringe.

'I know what you're saying, Cathie Gemmell!' he managed to gobble. 'We're as clean as you!'

'Come and play skips with us, Aggie!' wheedled Cathie. 'Never mind him!'

'The next time I have sweeties I'll give you some!' Aggie compromised with Eddie, and so the Kennys mingled again with the rest of them.

After that the morning passed more smoothly. Each pupil moved into his or her place in the school and the whole thing went forward like a giant team of horses, with Mrs McMinn cracking the whip behind to keep them from lagging. The efforts of the infants were praised, the mistakes of the others punished, and Cathie Gemmell, the best artist in the school, already had a drawing pinned to the wall.

'I'll take you for your singing lesson in the afternoon, Katherine,' the teacher said to Katy. 'I have a new song for you. It will be the very thing to sing to the Inspector! You never know, he may ask to hear someone sing. It's just as well to be prepared.'

Katy's singing voice was a rare thing which Mrs McMinn had welcomed with delight from the first day she stepped into the school and opened her mouth like a very young bird. The teacher tried to cultivate it when there was time, by giving her a few minutes of exercises up and down the scale, loudly and softly and with great patience.

'Oh, Rowan Tree!' was her best song and Katy sang it with so much feeling that the folk had to take out their hankies, and even Aggie's heart turned over.

In spite of Mrs McMinn's watchful eye Aggie managed to cast a furtive glance at the glass-doored bookcase below the statue of Our Lady, and saw it contained a few more books than before. That meant she would have something more now to read, for she never seemed to get enough books, and Ma got cross when she caught her reading the love story in the weekly paper, although she only read it to satisfy the craving to read that often came upon her.

At last the bell rang for the dinner-hour and she sighed with relief.

She was no good at drawing or singing and her arithmetic had to be worked at, but if, in the afternoon, Mrs McMinn gave her a composition to do, then she might show some merit, for the words she found impossible to utter came tumbling out on to the paper like the water from one of the hill springs.

At dinner-time the three girls went to Granda and Grandma Breen's in the Old Village to eat their 'pieces'. They were very lucky to be able to do this for most of the country ones at the other schools had to eat in the playground, summer and winter, with cold water from the tap to wash it down.

The grandparents lived in a low white cottage on the banks of the river. At one time they had farmed a croft and had brought up a large family who were all scattered except Auntie Lizzie, the youngest, and Ma.

Grandma was round and short with a small, lined face and blue eyes, that were very wise and kind. Aggie was said to resemble her and she believed this to be true for sometimes she could see her own face looking out of her grandmother's.

Granda Breen was bearded, with fierce bushy eyebrows.

When the girls entered the kitchen he greeted them with a loud roar and banged his stick, which he always kept handy, noisily on the floor.

'Ha, the Kennys!' he shouted, for he liked to be heard above everybody else. 'And how is the McMinn this day? Still battling on with that cane, I'll warrant ye!'

'She is that, Granda!' answered Katy whom Granda favoured. 'I got it once this morning!'

'You did!' Granda's stick banged more loudly in agitation. 'She might have controlled herself the first morning!'

'Here, you!' Grandma scolded as she poured out tea for the girls, now seated at the table. 'You control yourself! The whole place will hear you.'

'And who cares?' Granda roared back, resting his chin on his hands, crossed over the top of his stick.

Grandma smiled at Aggie as though sharing a secret. As long as Granda roared he was in the best of health and spirits and the whole family were happy.

A year or two ago when the war had just ended, things had been different. All the sons had come safely home except Thomas, one of the younger ones, who had been posted missing. Granda brooded and pined and took to his bed, silent and morose, while Grandma nursed him and went about her daily work just as before. When asked how she managed to keep so calm she replied that since she was married at sixteen, her faith had been tried many times and one more trial just had to be borne.

Then one morning early, Thomas came off the London train and stepped into the house, thin and ill from a prisoner-of-war camp, but whole and alive. Granda soon began to roar again.

After Grandma had poured the tea, she put her hand below her apron and nodded to Agnes. That meant she had a bag of sweets to slip to them on the way out. Granda did not believe in this for he liked to give big things, like the green woollen scarves they wore in the winter and Aggie's shepherd's tartan kilt, and their prayer books. To him small things were a waste of money, but Grandma knew that children get a lot of pleasure out of small things too.

'So your Aunt Lizzie is away visiting your Ma again today!' Granda suddenly said, speaking of his daughter as of a mere acquaintance.

'Ma is expecting her,' Aggie answered.

'Mm! She's away out there and that heathen of a Jamie Watson will go out to convoy her home at night!'

'Oh, but he doesn't always come right out, Granda,' Janey said innocently, and Aggie's eyes met Grandma's in alarm. 'He meets her up the road sometimes. I think Auntie Lizzie is like me. She's afraid in the dark!'

'Katy!' Granda roared. 'Throw a can of water over him! Two cans, if you get the chance! I'll have him christened!'

'I think it's about time you were getting back to the school, Agnes,' Grandma said, and her eyes were creased with laughter as she helped Janey off her chair. 'I'll see you all tomorrow again.'

The heat shimmered on the stone houses and the brown water ran low under the granite arches of the bridge, for it had been a dry summer. Now and again the leap of a trout disturbed the still surface of the river, but the trees along the banks, like their reflections in the water, were limp and motionless.

There were many of the High School girls about in the street, looking to Aggie very well dressed in navy blue blazers with gym tunics and white blouses.

'There's none of them got boots on!' Katy whispered to Aggie. 'And look at the books that one has in her bag! My, Aggie, if you have all that to learn!'

'The Qualifying isn't till next year!' Aggie answered with a shade of defiance in her tone. 'I have a long time yet,' and determined to put it out of her mind whenever she could.

'There's the big Nairn boy,' Janey said suddenly.

'So it is,' Katy replied. 'He called us names last year. We'd better hurry.'

'Sticks and stones will break my bones, but names will never hurt me,' recited Aggie. 'Give me your hand, Janey.'

They began to trot and some stones rattled at their heels as they raced through the schoolgate.

'I managed to put my tongue out at him,' panted Katy. 'Aggie, don't forget to give Eddie Campbell some of Grandma's sweeties.'

'I've got some for him,' her sister answered, as the bell rang. 'We'll take the rest home to Ma.'

Later in the afternoon when the school was over and they were back on the Big Road with the town well behind them, Aggie felt as though she had been gone for weeks, instead of just a day. It was still hot and the road was lumpy with tar blisters, but not far ahead lay the turning to the lane, where the high hedge gave shade and shelter and the dust lay soft and thick beneath the feet.

Aggie breathed deeply as they all sat down on the grassy bank on the side of the road where the harebells were growing. From the corn fields of the Home Farm near the Castle came the whirr of reapers and in the distance a bull bellowed loudly and in protest at the cows being taken into the byres for the milking.

'That's the first day past, thank goodness.' Katy groaned, and started to strip off her boots. 'It won't be that long till the Christmas holidays now!'

'Molly Riley is going to be my best friend,' Janey said, following her example. 'Aggie, will you carry my boots? Are you not taking yours off?'

Aggie shook her head.

'No, not just yet,' she answered. She had no notion of talking, and she did not want to pad along on her bare feet either. She would have had to keep her eyes on the road for stones and thorns instead of watching the roadsides for coloured leaves or brambles or bloody-men's-fingers.

She got up to go with Janey's school bag over her shoulder as well as her own. 'I'll carry your boots along with Janey's,' she said to Katy.

'Oh, hooray!' cried Katy, skipping through the dust, 'and whatever I find I'll give to you!'

The 'finds' were moss-roses from the hedge or acorns on a stem, and sprays of beech nuts from the Little Wood.

Aggie nodded. There was a blue haze over the valley and the Hill Village was faintly visible. But it was the smell she liked best. Today there was no mistaking the autumn smells, and the light wind mixed the scent of bracken from the hillsides with the pink and white clover that grew in the field where there had been a hay-crop earlier in the summer.

Under the trees of the Little Wood the shade was thick and green but the leaves had a dry rustle and some of them were already tinged with brighter hues.

Chapter Three

BY THE time August slipped into September Aggie had got back into the ways of Mrs McMinn. Sometimes in the school it seemed to her that she had never been out of them, and that the summer holidays had never happened. The road home at night always reassured her and the rumble of the harvest carts was the first thing she listened for coming down the lane.

The 'leading-in' of the corn was going steadily on for the fine weather held and each night she saw the fields a little barer. The days were shortening too, but there were still blackberries to be picked and most evenings Aggie set off round the fields with Ma's big enamel basin.

This night she decided to go up the ditch-side where the briars grew so thick and tangled in the hedge that the lane at the other side was completely hidden and the big juicy blackberries sprawled over the ditch.

When Aggie left the cottage the sun was still shining but the long pink and mauve clouds of evening were stretching across the sky in the west and the light was golden.

She had promised Ma that she would be home before darkening came down, and Auntie Lizzie, whose day it was for visiting, looked up from her knitting and said she would be leaving about then too.

As Aggie clambered along the ditch-side, she wondered if Jamie Watson would get as far as the cottage that night or not, or would he just meet Auntie Lizzie up the lane.

For as long as she could remember Jamie Watson had been coming to the house with Auntie Lizzie, and Ma had told her he had been coming long before that, as a boy, with Cousin John.

Jamie was a tall man, with fair hair and blue eyes, and quiet, steady ways. Everybody liked and respected him, even Granda Breen, in his own way, although he would never forgive him for not being christened.

Granda Breen believed in a man being God-fearing and obeying the laws of some church. No man could save his soul by himself; he needed the company of other people and the counsel of many. 'You can imagine,' he yelled at Grandma one day in Aggie's hearing, 'that the prayers of a hundred people are bound to have more effect than the prayers of one!'

'That depends.' Grandma replied.

'Depends! Depends on what?' he roared, nearly beside himself. 'Are you on Jamie Watson's side or mine?'

'Lizzie's,' she answered cheerfully.

Granda was stumped, for Auntie Lizzie had never defied him. She had accepted his decision that there would be no marriage unless Jamie was christened.

Jamie Watson's father had brought his son up to do what he thought was right both for himself and other people, and never mind the trimmings.

'Christening and all that is just a notion!' he told Jamie. 'I never had you christened and you're as good a man as the next. You keep your conscience clear, son, and never neglect your duty!'

Jamie's parents died and the Great War broke out. Jamie gave serious thought to his duty and made his decision. He closed down his cottage and joiner's business and joined up.

Each time he came back on leave he walked out in his uniform to Aggie's home along with Auntie Lizzie. They made a very splendid pair for she wore her best hat trimmed with pansies and her high-necked blouse with the frills.

When the war was over Jamie had come safely home and had started up his joinering as though he had never been away. He said himself that he had been very lucky and was thankful, for many a worthier man had not been spared.

It was Aggie's pride that Auntie Lizzie had stayed true to him for Aggie believed in love everlasting. And it was not that Auntie Lizzie lacked chances either, for there were plenty of men who went out of their way to be extra nice to Granda Breen when they saw him up at the market.

Of them all Wallie Johnstone was by far the best-looking. Handsome, black-haired and merry, he had a fine well-run little farm at the back of him and only poached because he liked it.

Auntie Lizzie was reckoned to be nice-looking too. She had a thick coil of red-brown hair piled at the back of her head, a clear skin and pink cheeks, and she walked straight and easy. She and Ma were great friends, although there was quite a difference in their ages since Ma was one of the oldest of the family.

Once and sometimes twice a week she came out to the cottage and spent the time mending and darning any of their clothes that needed it, and so it kept Ma from getting too far behind with the patching which never seemed to stop. These visits also gave Jamie Watson the chance of escorting her home.

The Great War had changed many things and among them were the fashions for women. Nowadays the ladies of the town wore much shorter skirts than they did before—Ma remembered when they nearly trailed on the ground—but Auntie Lizzie still clung to the longer ones, that went with pin-tucked blouses and wide sleeves, and her hats were big-brimmed and covered with velvet ribbons and flowers.

Sometimes of late Aggie imagined that Ma was just a bit

worried about Auntie Lizzie for it was a good long time now since she was sixteen. When any of the other girls round about got married these days, Ma hardly ever talked about it, and Aggie could clearly remember the time when the details of every wedding were gone over a dozen times, from the bride's blossom to the friends that had not been asked.

The thought of Ma reminded Aggie that she had promised not to stay out too late. The sun had now set and dusk was beginning to fall. A white mist was settling over the fields and evening was bringing out the heavy dews and the coolness that came with the first breath of autumn.

Setting down the basin of berries she seated herself on the bank with her hands round her knees.

'I'll stay for just a minute,' she told herself.

The air was still for the harvesting was over for that day. A humclock droned by and from the stackyard up at the farm came the sound of men's voices and the barking of a dog.

'I wish the summer was just starting!' Aggie sighed. 'I wish—I wish it never ended.'

It had been a fine dry summer and the harvest was early, with the carting-in of the corn well ahead. It was not always like this for Ma had told of wet summers when the blackened sheaves were still lying out in the fields at the end of October.

But this had been a blessed year. The corn had grown high and straight, and to lie on the edge of the field and peer into the forest of cornstalks was like looking at another world. Little coloured pansies bloomed there, yellow, mauve and white, scarlet pimpernels and blue-eyes, and gowans and green creepers; small beetles and 'red soldiers' and long-legged spiders moved about in that secret land and paid no heed to the wind rustling the heads of corn far above them.

'I wonder what they do now in the stubble!' Aggie thought with a frown. 'It's so bare!'

'Agnes! Agnes! Time you were home!' Ma's voice rang out from the cottage door some way down the lane, and then followed a murmur of voices.

'That's Auntie Lizzie going back to the town,' thought Aggie. 'I'll call to her through the hedge.'

Listening to the 'Good-nights' and the small talk in between, she then heard Auntie Lizzie's steps coming along the lane.

Next she heard another set of footsteps which made her stay quite still. Someone was walking slowly and deliberately down the lane the other way.

Aggie held her breath as the steps came nearer and almost jumped out of her skin the next second when a man's voice came out of the dusk.

'Is that you, Lisbeth?'

'Aye, Jamie, it's me!' Auntie Lizzie's voice answered. 'Have you been waiting?'

'No. I have just come!'

Both voices were now opposite Aggie on the other side of the hedge, but the twilight was too deep and the hedge too thick to see anything. Also now she did not dare get up and move away as it would look queer her being there at all.

'They'll think I sat here to listen,' she thought to herself. 'And there's a cramp in my leg now. I can't move!'

There was a moment's silence, then a light smack and Auntie Lizzie said: 'Oh, Jamie!' loud enough for Aggie to hear.

'Goodness!' she thought in astonishment, 'I believe Auntie Lizzie let Jamie kiss her!'

'Any news?' the man then asked.

'News? Jamie, what news could there be?' Auntie Lizzie answered rather sadly.

'Oh, I just thought that maybe your father . . .'

'My father, Jamie, will never change his mind till you change yours. That you know!'

'Oh, Lisbeth! It's a terrible problem. My own father was that much against christening, I can't bring myself to defy him. He was such a good-living man!' He paused. 'And I've said all this before,' he added. 'You'll be tired hearing it!'

'That's not the way I see it, Jamie,' Auntie Lizzie replied

39

with some spirit in her voice. 'Your father had his own opinions. They suited him, you are entitled to yours.'

'I wish I could persuade myself to that way of thinking, Lisbeth. And I've kept ye waiting a long time and the house and all is there. I'm sorry, Lisbeth,' and his voice was humble.

'I'll wait a wee while longer,' sighed Auntie Lizzie. 'I have no choice. You know my father's views.'

'I think he's just a bit hard on us, Lisbeth!' Jamie said. 'Meaning no disrespect,' he added.

'He's thinking of me, that's all. He thinks that a marriage stands a better chance if the couple are of the same opinion.'

'There's something in that,' agreed Jamie.

'Here. Lisbeth!' and there was another smack.

'That's twice,' Aggie breathed to herself, as she cautiously stretched her leg. 'He kissed her twice and he called her Lisbeth, but he says Lizzie in the house just like us!'

'Agnes! Agnes! Come on here at once! Your father will be home any minute.'

Ma's voice was loud and stern.

'That's my sister calling Agnes in,' Auntie Lizzie said. 'She's picking berries round the fields. We'll better be away too, Jamie. We have a good way to go yet!' and their footsteps slowly moved off.

Aggie got up carefully. She was cramped and cold for the grass was already wet with dew. Picking up the basin of blackberries she walked slowly along the field-side. It was nearly dark, but here in the fields she felt no fear. On the road it was different. Many a time on her way to the town alone she had slipped behind a hedge or the dike until someone she did not know had passed. Tonight only the bats were out and they squeaked and fluttered about like swallows in the daytime. From the Far Orchard came the hoot of an owl and a bird twittered uneasily in the hedge as a prowling cat or a weasel disturbed its rest.

Carefully climbing the gate she stepped on to the lane into the shaft of light that came from the open door.

'Agnes, you know I don't like you out in the dark,' Ma greeted her. 'Did you not hear me calling you?'

'Yes, Ma, I did, but I was just coming,' she replied, feeling guilty and not daring to explain. 'I got a lot of berries. See!'

'Oh, so you have. I'll boil them tomorrow. They'll be coming to an end soon!'

'There's still a lot up the ditch-side.'

'Aye, but once the morning frost gets them they taste different! Come on in now. Your father and the boys will be home soon. They'll be very tired for it has been a long day. Katy and Janey are in their beds.'

Aggie followed Ma into the kitchen where a bright fire was burning.

'You did all your lessons, didn't you, Agnes?' Ma asked, turning the wick of the lamp up a little.

'Yes, Ma! Sums and spelling. I did them early!'

'That's a good lass. You'd better eat something before you go to your bed. You're growing fast!'

Aggie helped herself to some bread and butter and a cup of milk and sat down at the fireside opposite Ma. A pot of oatmeal porridge simmered on the hob and now and then Ma leaned forward to stir it with the serious look of someone who thought the making of good porridge a very important thing.

'Ma,' asked Aggie suddenly, 'how long has Jamie been courting Auntie Lizzie?'

'Oh. Many a year now,' Ma answered, staring into the fire. 'Far too long at that! It's time now . . .'

'Time! Time for what, Ma?' asked Aggie eagerly.

'Time you were in your bed too!' Ma replied sharply. 'You have to wash yourself yet. Face, neck, feet and knees. Hurry up now!'

There was no mistaking the command in Ma's voice this time and Aggie went into the back pantry where a candle flickered on the mealark. A small zinc tin of lukewarm water stood ready and she set too as quickly as possible with the carbolic soap. She had to hurry for the water had to be changed for Da and the boys and that meant Ma had to fetch more water from the pump.

The pump stood at the field gate across the lane and all the water used had to be carried into the house. Andrew Blackwell said the time would come when the law would insist that every house had the water inside, running from taps.

'It will be a while yet, mind you,' he had added. 'The country will take some time to get over the war.'

But it gave Ma new hope and she sometimes talked of 'when we get the water in' just the way Aggie and her sister said 'when we get our holidays'.

She had just finished and Ma had brought fresh water when Da and the boys came into the kitchen, their heavy boots making a great clatter on the stone floor.

'Is that you, Agnes?' Da said to her, hanging up his cap behind the door. 'Isn't it time you were in your bed?'

'I'm just going, Da,' she replied, padding over the red tiles in her bare feet, her boots and stockings in her hand.

'Did ye get on all right at the school?' he stood for a moment and looked at her.

'Oh, yes. The teacher caught Bernie Jones making faces, and he got two on each hand!'

'Oh, dear! Any news in the town?'

Aggie thought for a second to try to remember anything that Grandma might have said.

'No, Da,' she shook her head.

'There's never any news,' grumbled John, a tall fairhaired boy with down on his face. 'Aggie, you're lucky still to be at the school! I'm fair tired. It's been a long day!'

'Harvest days are aye long days,' Da answered, going into the pantry to wash. 'You'll feel better after your porridge!'

'I think I'll wash at the pump to save time,' was John's only comment as he went to fetch a bucket from the lobby.

'Leave the bucket, will you, John?' Robert called out, settling himself down by the fireside. 'I'll wash there too, when you've finished.'

'Robert,' Aggie asked, taking the chance of Ma talking to Da in the pantry, 'did you find anything today?'

Her brother raised his head, which was dark like Ma's.

'You'd better go on to your bed, Aggie, before Ma catches ye!' he warned her in the quiet voice that was like Da's, only deeper.

'I'm just going! I just wondered if you saw anything in the harvest field,' she insisted.

'Plenty of rabbits, and a hare. The nests of some fieldmice below the stooks!'

'Oh, the poor things! I expect they got an awful fright,' and for a moment her mind was filled with the thought of a harassed family of mice, scurrying through the stubble, looking for shelter. 'Robert, tell Da to call me early, I have all the boots to clean.' And she set off along the lobby.

'I'll not forget,' Robert answered.

Setting her boots beside those of her two sisters, Aggie undressed by the light of the candle burning on top of the chest-of-drawers. Then she knelt down by the side of the bed and said the 'Our Father'. Sometimes she said more prayers than that, but she never missed that one, as Grandma said it had everything in it a body needed if you looked at it close enough.

Aggie never got any of the holy notions that attacked Katy now and again, when she went about with one of Ma's aprons round her head and said she was a nun. Sometimes too she held church services with Janey for the congregation. Then she went through the whole service with the sermon, the choir and the collection all there, and a bunch of old keys tied to a piece of string for an incense-burner. Da had remarked there was hardly any need to go to church as long as Katy lived with them.

After the cold floors it was warm and cosy in bed next to Katy and Janey who were both asleep. There was a murmur of voices from the kitchen and the splashing of water from the pump outside where the boys were washing.

43

Then she heard them come back into the house, first John, then Robert, and the door was closed for the night.

There was no sound outside now, except for the soft sigh of the hawthorn hedge that sheltered the north side of the house. All would be still and quiet in the fields and the Far Orchard and the river banks. Unless Wallie Johnstone was out. Everybody knew Wallie was a poacher, even the gamekeeper, who had never yet been able to catch him at it. Several times when Robert and John had taken Aggie along with them on their rambles over the fields, they had shown her the cunningly placed snares and traps.

'Wallie Johnstone's been here!' they told her as they snapped the traps with a stick. 'It's a pity for anything caught in these teeth!'

Now lying in bed with the darkness all round the house, she thought of Wallie slipping over the wet grass through the night. Or would it be the early morning when he went poaching?

Then she remembered Jamie Watson kissing Auntie Lizzie up in the lane. She had read in the paper about folk kissing each other and she once heard Nathan Thomson say that the laird had tried to kiss the lady-post during the war, when she went to the Castle with the letters.

Here in the south-west nobody did much kissing except the lovers and they tried hard not to let anybody see them. She was aware of Ma coming into the room and saying something as she tucked in the bedclothes. Then it was darkness.

It was a heavisome thing for all that to see the summer passing. The sun still shone from a hazy sky during the day but the mists and dews fell heavier at night.

Aggie picked the last of the blackberries and climbed the twisted old apple trees in the Far Orchard to shake down the sour green apples that Ma turned into jelly.

The shelf of home-made jam in the pantry was well covered for Ma made jam of all the fruit that came her way. There was plenty of rhubarb for it grew in the garden, and the jam made from it was rich dark brown with little bits of ginger here and there. The plums came from Miss Blackwell's orchard, the blackcurrants from Mrs McClurg's who lived over in the Hill Village, and the gooseberries from a bush that grew wild along the river bank.

This year too, there was raspberry, for there was such a big crop in the Castle garden that the laird had sent word that one of the boys could go and pick enough for a boiling. Aggie did not expect to taste much of the raspberry jam for it was kept for visitors like Mrs McMinn and the friends from Glasgow.

Ma enjoyed having visitors since she never could go very far herself, as she always had to come back for the milking. The next best thing, after having folk in the house, however, was to watch them pass by in the lane. On the fine Sunday evenings of the summer she and Da would sit out on the wooden seat in the sun, for the front of the house got the sun most of the day. From there in all seasons a never-ending pageant of light and cloud passed by for the house stood flatly in the middle of the Little Valley and the sky looked high and wide.

Occasionally a few of the townsfolk took their Sunday walk along the lane for there were wild flowers to be picked in the roadside grass and fine long switches in the hedges for the flies.

When some of them were sighted Aggie and Katy and Janey sat down on the seat beside Ma and kept looking very properly the other way, so that nobody could say they were staring.

Sometimes the passers-by greeted the Kennys and sometimes not, for some of the townsfolk thought themselves superior to the country folk—when the latter knew it to be the other way round—and they passed on by, the silence broken only by the squeaky jerks of their Sunday boots.

If there were children with the party it was all the better, for as soon as they saw the pump they all wanted a drink of water. Then Ma and Da held a little polite conversation while Aggie took the chance to look at what they all wore.

'That girl is just my age!' Katy would whisper. 'She's got on a pink silk frock! Real silk!'

'I like the straw hat with the blue streamers!' said Janey.

'Don't point!' hissed Aggie. 'She's looking at us!'

In the meantime the people were moving off with many a backward glance at the cottage with the pink ramblers in bloom and the row of pansies in the border.

The shortening of the days put an end to the long walks of the townsfolk and there were few blooms left on the ramblers. Aggie had little time for 'raking' the countryside as Ma called it, like she had done in the long summer evenings with Robert or John, for Mrs McMinn saw that she had plenty of homework and it was dark when she had finished it.

Then the heat haze of September thickened into cool grey clouds, hiding the face of the sun, which sent its long streamers, like silver fingers, poking down into the bay.

By the time the harvest moon was into her third quarter, the fields were bare and the swallows had gone.

Chapter Four

THE cornstacks had still to be thatched so Da and the boys went down to the river edge and mowed great swathes of reeds. At the same time they gathered up the driftwood and trees cast up by the water when in flood, to be brought home later for winter burning.

After the thatching of the stacks the sides of the hedges were trimmed and the air was filled with the smell of the smoke from the fires made to burn the cuttings.

From the trees in the Little Wood the first of the leaves began to drift quietly down and then a west wind came and tormented the trees. The leaves came spinning through the air like flights of birds and the lane was ankle-deep in the red and gold rustle.

'This is nearly as nice as the summer,' Katy remarked as they collected the coloured leaves and branches of hips and haws for Mrs McMinn. 'I like when we get nature study. It's a change from the lessons. And you know what Granda says about the arithmetic?'

'No, Katy. What does he say?' enquired Janey.

'That arithmetic's new-fangled. If you can count your money, that's enough!'

47

Aggie giggled. She knew that Katy was much quicker-witted than herself and was no plodder, but she had a pertness that could make them all laugh, which was a good thing for she herself was too serious.

Aggie liked the tangy smell of autumn, the smoke and wet leaves smell, and the veil of mist that lay over the hills and the Little Valley, giving an air of mystery to the land. She liked the stillness that enveloped the days from the golden haze of the early morning sunshine, to the mauve dusks, when the steadings up at the Big Farm seemed to fade away into the darkness.

The long struggle from the spring through the summer was ended.

There were other things now on the country road. Squirrels raced along the branches of the trees or stared at them with unblinking eyes as they passed by; a solitary blackbird chuckled anxiously in the hedge where last year's nests stood revealed; overhead whirred an arrow of geese southwards to the bay. On the clear days when the mists rolled away for a spell, the sides of Barrhill and Larg stood revealed in their rich autumn colours, but Cairnsmore-of-Fleet kept to his own shade of blue.

It was a good year for chestnuts. Every morning Aggie and her sisters raced to reach the Chestnut Wood to pick up what had fallen during the night and Eddie Campbell and Tom Riley and the other boys could hardly wait for the morning break to see if Aggie had any to spare for them.

At night time Robert strung Janey's into a big necklace which she took to school with her in her bag. After the school was over she put them round her neck much to Katy's shame, who said everybody was looking at her.

This was because the shopkeeper at the foot of the school hill had warned Janey that 'she had better watch out and not trip over her pearls', for the string dangled to her knees. Janey bit her lip and looked at Aggie, who saw the anxious appeal in her little sister's face.

'Keep them on if you like them!' was Aggie's answer, although she herself would never have dared wear them.

'I think they're silly!' Katie said huffily, walking on, but after a few minutes she turned round and said she would carry Janey's schoolbag. Janey wore the chestnut necklace until it was old and withered and the chestnut time had passed.

One Sunday, early in October, Mrs McMinn caught hold of John after church and told him that evening classes were starting in the school in the Old Village and that he ought to go. 'Yes, ma'am,' John answered sheepishly, trying to be agreeable and wishing he had got away sooner.

'You may wish later on that you had kept up your education. After all, you may not want to spend the rest of your life working on a farm!' she insisted, and the feathers in her Sunday hat bobbed in emphasis.

'Please, ma'am, there's no other work!' John said gruffly, for his voice was half-way through breaking.

'No, John, perhaps not just now, but what about later on? Have you ever thought of the Police Force? Of course, you're not nearly age for that yet, but you are a fine healthy boy and tall for your age. You'll probably grow more yet. If I were you I'd go to the evening classes. A person can never know enough anyway! Perhaps Robert will go with you.'

Aggie, who stood waiting for John, said to Katy later that she had never seen her brother look so pleased before.

'He pulled back his shoulders, and his face went red, and he showed all his teeth as though the teacher had given him a present, instead of a lecture about going back to the school. And then he shouted "yes, ma'am!" I was glad everybody was away from the church door!'

Aggie had to stride to keep up with John for the rest of the family were well ahead, and he was in a hurry to tell Da about the night school and the Police Force, it being Ma's Sunday at home.

'Well, I must say it's very kind of the teacher!' Da said,

49

when he heard it, 'but you have a good while to go yet before you're age to be a policeman!'

'I know that,' John answered, 'but I can wait.'

'Oh, well, if you can walk the distance to the town twice a week, after your day's work, you can please yourself!' Da replied. 'When I was a young man I thought nothing of walking five miles to a dancing class!'

Aggie had heard this before. Ma had told her once that when Da was young, there was not a better dancer at the kirns and barn dances than he. The war had put a stop to all these gatherings for most of the men were away, and although now it was over, habits were changing and new ways were replacing the old.

'You can take the bike!' Robert said, 'for I have no notion of the evening classes. I mean to stick to the land, anyway.'

'A bit extra learnin' will not hurt ye, Robert!' Da pointed out. 'Katy, lift your feet! You'll soon have no boots left!'

'No, I know!' Robert replied with a touch of stubbornness, 'but I'd feel a bit old among the rest!'

'Maybe so!' Da agreed.

At home Ma listened as she ladled out the barley broth that she made most Sundays, and Aggie caught the light of interest that showed in her face immediately. She had seen that look before when Mrs McMinn had started on about the Qualifying.

'What do you think, Da?' she asked meekly, like she always did, but Aggie knew fine that her mind was made up already. John would go to the night-school whatever anybody said or did.

On the first night he set out, they all went to the door to see him off. It was a dry starless night and very dark, and for a moment Aggie watched the glow of the carbide lamp bobbing up and down in the lane, then disappearing into the Hollow. She shivered and ran back into the well-lit kitchen.

'He'll make a fine policeman if he sticks in!' Ma remarked and then added with a sigh 'A few years is not long going past, and I don't think John is much taken with working with horses!'

'There will soon be one horse less up at the Farm, anyway.' Da said, settling back into his chair.

'Oh? Which one will that be?' Ma asked.

'Big Charlie. The master says he'll try and sell him at the horse sale. That'll be a fortnight come Saturday. The October market is next Friday!'

'Big Charlie!' The three girls looked at Da and each other. 'Big Charlie!' they repeated.

'Aye. The same!' Da answered.

'Oh, but that's a shame. Big Charlie has been here since he was a foal,' said Katy.

'Maybe so, but he still belongs to Mr Blackwell.' Da sighed as he picked up the paper and Aggie knew better than to say any more.

'I believe the master thinks he's too big and wild for us to handle!' Robert ventured.

October was the month for the sheep and cattle sales with the big market in the second week, the hiring day for the November term. Last year Ma had kept Aggie and her sisters off the school and had taken them into the town on the market day. The streets were full of people who had come from the outlying places and villages and all the way up the town Ma was stopping to talk to people she had known in the past.

Everybody was in fine humour, for the harvest was over and a man could go and have a dram while the women chatted about their families and friends and the days when they were all young.

'You've three fine girls there too, Mrs Kenny!' they always said. At this Janey immediately hid behind Ma's skirt and Aggie could feel the red blush creeping over her own face. It was left to Katy to give a quick bright smile, still being too shy to speak, with the result that she very often received a sixpence or so to divide with her sisters.

'The country ones!' Aggie often thought of herself. 'I wish

51

I didn't blush when anybody looked at me! I wish folk wouldn't look at me at all!'

Up at the market-place the cattle sales were going on and the noise was deafening because opposite the cattle pens was the field where the shows were doing brisk business.

It was Aggie's first time at the shows and the music and the glitter was something she could not find words to describe. All the show folk were dressed in bright colours and the women at the shooting stalls and dolly-shots wore golden earrings and diamond necklaces that sparkled and shone brighter than anything Aggie had ever seen.

'I don't think they'll be real diamonds, Agnes!' Ma remarked when Aggie mentioned this to her.

'Oh, but they are, Ma!' Katy burst in. 'You can tell by the way they dazzle you!'

Ma held her tongue and gave them money to have a ride on the roundabouts. There was little money to spend at the shows, as they knew, and they had been told to keep something to buy one of the little toy tanks or cannons that the ex-servicemen were selling on the street.

'It's a damned shame!' Aggie heard a passer-by remark, 'that a man coming home from the trenches should have to do this for a living!'

'They say it's worse in the big towns,' somebody said to Ma. 'There, there's neither work nor money.'

'It's always the same after a war,' a woman who knew Ma said. 'My two sons are talking of emigrating to Canada. There's plenty of land out there and work as well. I'll miss them awfully. It's so far away if anything happens.'

'It is a long way!' Ma agreed with sympathy in her voice. 'But I've heard of many that went out and did very well.'

'That's true enough!' the other answered. 'And there's nothing worse than seeing young men idling away their lives without a job. Ye've three fine girls there, Mrs Kenny. And where are your boys?'

'They set off with their father. They're likely in the market field. Maybe you'll run into them there. I've got to get back home now for the milking.'

On the way home the light wind carried the music of the roundabouts in faint gusts behind them right out along the road and Aggie found it very tantalizing.

This year Ma said there was to be no staying at home from the school for the market.

'Oh, Ma. We never get anywhere,' Aggie complained. 'Mrs McMinn will never miss us for a day!'

'I promised Mrs McMinn that I'd do my best to keep your attendance regular this year, Agnes,' Ma replied. 'To give you every chance for your examination.'

'That's but right.' Da interrupted. 'The woman herself has to have the same chance, Agnes, and she can't teach ye if you're not there. So let's hear no more about it.'

Da's word was final so Aggie just had to forget about the market and think of something else. This was easy enough when she remembered about the horse sale which lay just ahead, for that was when Big Charlie was due to go.

The Farm would not be the same without the big horse, for ever since he was a foal, he had been a character.

'There's nothing vicious about him,' Da always said. 'He just doesn't know his own strength. He never seems to get tired!'

Where another horse walked, Big Charlie trotted, and when the other cantered, he galloped, and when he was between the shafts of a farm cart, he pulled it like it was a chariot.

On the day of the horse sale after Ma came home from the byre, Aggie raced up the lane in the fresh October morning to see the last of Big Charlie.

For some time she waited in the lea of the hedge near the farmyard, listening to the rattle of harness and milkcans and the swilling of water. Then Da came out of the stable with the end of a halter dangling over his shoulder and Big Charlie dancing along behind it.

53

Aggie had a lump in her throat when she saw him. He had been curried and groomed until his chestnut coat gleamed and shone; his tail was plaited and his mane hung like a fringe of fawn silk.

Andrew Blackwell appeared out of the byre. 'Oh, my, he does look well!' he remarked to Da, looking the horse over. 'It's a pity he's so wild!'

Hooking his thumbs into his waistcoat armholes he stared at the horse heavily for a moment and then added abruptly: 'Oh, well, David, you go on in to the mart and I'll follow on the bike when I've finished the byres. The boys can leave when they've fed the beasts.'

Da waved a hand to Aggie and went on up the lane with the horse trotting behind. Aggie watched them till they disappeared round the bend and sometimes she saw the horse put his big head over her father's shoulder and a hand reached up to stroke him.

Any other Saturday Aggie was only too pleased to be at home with Ma and her sisters, and the day passed far too uickly. This day it was different.

After the grocer with his horse-van had called, the postman came by and handed in a letter from Grandma Kenny. In long, sloping, careful handwriting she said they were all in their usual and hoped that her son, daughter and family were the same.

Aggie and Katy then made the beds and swept the floors and Robert and John came in to change their clothes to go to the town.

'Be careful up at the market!' Ma warned them, for on days like this, a little money could be made by young men, holding horses until their owners went to get some dinner or a drink. They were nearly ready and Ma had begun the baking, when the sound of a man singing and a horse trotting took Aggie and Katy to the door.

'That's Hughie Grant, the milk-tester!' said Katy eagerly. 'I hope he stops!'

The singing came nearer and a brown pony came into

view drawing a high gig on which sat a good-looking young man. It stopped abruptly in front of the house.

'Whoa, there, Nancy lass! Whoa there! Anybody for the horse sale?' he called out. 'Jump up, you two!'

'Oh, we're not going!' Katy answered with a sigh. 'Just the boys. And Da's away with Big Charlie!'

'So I heard. And I'm disappointed once again!'

'Had we never met nor parted, We would ne'er been broken-hearted,' he recited to them with a grin.

The boys climbed up beside him and with a wave and a 'Gee-up, Nancy! Gee-up there!' they were off.

As Aggie dusted the ornaments on the dresser she listened to Ma getting worried because John was growing out of his best clothes.

'He'll get new ones when the pig's killed,' she said, 'but that's not for another six weeks. Thank goodness, Robert's are still a good fit!'

The thought of John's jacket had no worry for Aggie, but the pig had, and now and again she took a race round the corner of the house just to let him know he had some friends.

'Hullo, Henry!' she called out, and there was a concert of squeals and grunts in reply.

The hens, whose coops were along the hedge-side in the field at the back of the house, she never went near. They were Ma's special friends and she talked to them the way some folk talk to their bees. Besides, although the big white cockerel strutted round Ma, he thought nothing of giving anybody else a lightning peck on the leg when he got the chance.

In the afternoon Aggie perched herself on top of the gate on the other side of the lane. She could see as far as Miss Blackwell's farm up the way but down the way the lane twisted and turned between the high hedges, coming very close to the river at one place, and then it curved east to join the Big Road farther on.

Above and around was the wide stretch of sky, grey and

overcast today, but never failing to give Aggie that fine feeling of scope. The Hill Village, clinging to the hillside slopes, seemed a long way off, and Cairnsmore was shrouded in mist.

Now and again in the still quiet air, she heard the clipclop of horses' hooves along the Big Road and the whirr of a motor-car. The earth was quiet too, and the land was sleeping. Soon the ploughing would begin and the green sod would be turned over to let the dark earth feel the light.

At the bottom of the hedges the ivy trailed its dark green branches, where the ferns were turning brown, but a small white flower, like a starry speck, still bloomed among the greenery.

For some time Aggie watched the young stirks romping in the field, by the river, near the Far Orchard. They raced about like children, running half-way down the field, then stopping abruptly and running back. Then suddenly they seemed to tire of the game and they all began cropping the grass, keeping close together in a little herd as if for company.

By and by Aggie heard faint voices and footsteps from far up the lane, beyond the farmhouse. She listened keenly. There were men talking together and the smart sound of a trotting horse.

'Ma!' she called out. 'Katy and Janey! I think Big Charlie's back.'

Without waiting for an answer she raced up the lane and reached the farm as Da and the boys came forward along with Mr Blackwell, wheeling his bike.

Behind them trotted Big Charlie as lively as ever.

'Nobody would buy him!' the master called out to her before she could ask. 'So we had to bring him back.'

'I'll never know why you took him in the first place,' Miss Blackwell answered him as she came out of the little white gate in front of the house.

'Now, Jessie, you know fine I don't want anybody to get hurt,' her brother replied. 'That horse never takes his time! He just prances on! Robert, let him loose in the field.'

They all watched as the big horse cantered through the gate, and when it shut behind him, he turned to look at them; then he shook his head, neighed loudly and shrilly and set off at a gallop round the field.

They all had to laugh.

'That's that!' was Mr Blackwell's comment as he blew his nose. 'It looks as though Big Charlie will be mine for the rest of his days!'

'He's always biddable to me,' said Da firmly. 'I would have been sorry to see him go.'

'I'm kind of glad to see him back myself,' the farmer agreed. 'Jessie, if you had seen the look he gave some of the folk that came near him!' He laughed.

'Very likely,' Miss Blackwell commented drily. 'He would be having a day out like the rest of you.'

On the way home John told Aggie that he had never seen so many motor-cars as had been in the town that day.

'Some day,' he said, 'folk will not want horses, because they're too slow! Everybody will have a motor!'

'How can you say that, John!' Aggie argued. 'Look how Prince takes us to the Cattle Show. Just look at Big Charlie!'

'It doesn't matter,' insisted John. 'It'll turn out like I say.'

'You're worse than Katy!' Aggie said back, and there was a queer hurt feeling inside her. 'She's just like you, always reading in the paper about aeroplanes trying to fly to America and they never get there! I don't like motor-cars *or* aeroplanes!'

'You've never been in any of them!' mocked her brother as they reached the house.

With Big Charlie safely back, Aggie could now look forward to Hallowe'en without any fear of sad feelings rising up to spoil it all. The weather was growing colder with boisterous winds that seemed determined to strip the last leaves from the trees; the oaks and the beeches clung firmly to theirs, as to the ragged remnants of a cloak that fluttered drily when the wind shook the tatters. On the clear and sunny days the woods and the hillsides glowed with rich colours and the distant hills were violet; when the rain fell the lane was filled with water holes in which anybody could see the heavens without raising a head.

'Agnes!' Mrs McMinn said one afternoon, 'after this you and Katherine and Mary Jane may put away your books at half-past three and leave so that you are home before dark.'

'Yes, ma'am!' answered Aggie, much relieved, although she had been expecting this, for the country ones were allowed out early in the winter months.

They were hurrying along the Big Road when a car honked behind them, and drew to a stop. It was the Doctor in his new two-seater.

'Get in, the three of you!' he yelled above the noise of the engine, as he flung the door open. 'Here, Katy, you first, and then the young one. Agnes, you'll be sitting sideways, but never mind, as long as you're in. Hup! We're away!'

It was the first time that any of them had ever been in a motor-car and Aggie had never felt a sensation like it. It was smoother than the train journey to Grandma Kenny's and there was not the jogging of the spring-cart like there was behind a horse, although the doctor spoke to his engine as he spoke to the pony he had had all his life up to now.

'Gently now! Easy does it!' he said, as the car left the Big Road and slid into the lane, where it began to bounce among the potholes. Katy uttered a squeal of delight and the doctor's grey moustache twitched in his lean red face.

'This is the worst road in the country!' he roared at Aggie. 'I hear you're going to the High School.'

'I have to pass the Qualifying first,' she shouted back.

'You'll pass,' said the doctor firmly, giving her a swift, shrewd glance. 'You have enough brains and the McMinn behind you with the cane! And then you'll learn to think, and heaven help you when you learn to think!'

'Mrs McMinn says we should always stop and think,' gasped Katy from somewhere below Janey.

The doctor's face broke into a wide smile. 'Just tell her that the next time she wants to cane you! But she's a fine woman, is Mrs McMinn. Just like your Auntie Lizzie. When is the wedding coming off?'

'We don't know. She has to wait for Jamie's christening.'

'Huh.' That'll be the day! Whoa there!' grunted the doctor, as they drew up in front of the farmhouse. 'I'll just pop in to see Jessie Blackwell's leg before she calls me out in six feet of snow. My regards to your mother and father!' and with a playful pat on Aggie's shoulder, who was trying to mumble her thanks, he grasped his bag and strode off into the house.

'Aggie!' Janey chattered on the way down the lane, 'I wish we had a motor-car!'

'You need a lot of money for a motor-car!' said Katy sharply. 'An awful lot of money! The doctor has to have a motor to visit the sick folk. We don't!'

'Aggie, Katy's cross,' Janey called out in surprise.

'I'm not cross, I only wish Jamie Watson would get christened. Everybody's asking us.' Katy answered, and she looked a disconsolate little figure as she trudged on ahead.

'But we can't help it, Ma says it's nothing to do with us,' Aggie tried to remind her.

'I know that,' replied Katy, turning round. 'But they ask just the same. Eddie Campbell said yesterday that Jamie was just afraid of getting his head wet!'

'Oh, so is Eddie, by the look of him,' Aggie retorted. 'and his face as well!'

This made them all giggle and Katy's good humour returned, and then the sight of Ma coming round the end of the house made them forget about it.

'Ma!' Janey called, and beginning to run, 'we had a ride in the doctor's motor! In the doctor's new motor, Ma.'

But several nights later when Miss Blackwell took them into the parlour for their Hallowe'en—after insisting that she did not know them, disguised as they were in false faces and the boys' clothes—the subject cropped up again.

Andrew Blackwell was sitting by the fire with some lady visitors from the town, when the girls trooped in and Aggie went through some dreadful minutes because the rubber soles of her Sunday boots squeaked on the polished floor with every step she took.

'Ha! Three young fellows come for their Hallowe'en!' the farmer greeted them, and the other ladies looked at them with great amusement. 'First, they have to entertain us, of course, as is the custom!' and he leaned back in his chair with an expectant air. 'And then we'll see!'

Coming up the lane along with John who was waiting for them outside the gate in the dark, they had agreed that Aggie should say her piece first, with Janey second, and Katy would come last, for she had something special to offer.

'Oh, Mary, go and call the cattle home!' she announced, and cleared her throat.

She had chosen this because it was short and also Da liked it too. She spoke loud and clear for it was easier to recite behind a false face than with a bare face.

Everybody clapped when she had finished and then Janey followed with 'Two little clouds one summer day'.

Aggie now thought this a fine chance to have a good look at the parlour. She had been in it several times already so she knew where to start looking. There was the piano set cornerwise and the bookcases in the wall at each side of the fireplace, and the two big armchairs and the sofa covered with cloth that had a pattern of faded pink roses all over it. Against another wall stood a cupboard, with a glass door, which Ma had told them was called a cabinet. Through the glass could be seen silver and china ornaments and a row of flowery cups and saucers that seemed too good to use. Aggie sighed to herself. Such a cupboard would be a nice change from the dresser at home, but then they had no parlour to put it in and Ma always had willow pattern for it was easy to match.

A nudge from Katy brought her back to earth for she always seemed to know when Aggie's attention was wandering.

Janey had stopped reciting and it was now Katy's turn.

'Oh, Rowan Tree!' she announced and clasping her hands behind her back she raised her head and began to sing.

Aggie was used to Katy's singing. She had sung since she was very small and Cousin John had taught her 'We're all jolly fellows' before she knew the meaning of the words. The interest that the teacher took in her voice made no difference to Katy's own outlook—she liked to sing to people she knew, but was very shy before strangers. But this was Hallowe'en. Tonight she was expected to sing and, like her sister, the mask she wore increased her confidence.

Aggie turned to watch what Katy's singing was doing to the other people and as the clear sweet voice rang out she saw at once that the listeners were caught up in its magic. When she came to the high notes in the line 'Thy leaves are aye the first o' spring' Aggie's own heart turned over and Andrew Blackwell closed his eyes and rested his chin on his chest.

Aggie then looked at the ladies, for the wearing of a false face allowed her many liberties and the ladies could not know she was staring at them either. The expression on all their faces was one of soft and tender memory and Aggie felt satisfied.

When the song ended there was a minute's stillness and then Andrew Blackwell cleared his throat and said loudly: 'Only Katy Kenny can sing like that! Jessie, give them all a good Hallowe'en!'

With that the ladies started to talk and pass remarks about Katy's voice and then they got out their purses.

Aggie tried to steal another look round the parlour for among the ornaments in the cabinet was one of the country boy looking for a thistle on the sole of one of his bare feet.

Once more Katy gave her a sharp nudge and she realized that Miss Blackwell was handing out apples and nuts and one of the ladies was giving them each a shilling.

'I know your grandparents in the Old Village,' she said. 'And your Auntie Lizzie too. Any word of her getting married?'

Aggie swallowed. It was quite true what Katy had said. Everybody was asking.

'I don't know, ma'am,' she replied politely.

'She'll better not wait too long!' Andrew Blackwell said. 'or she'll end like Jessie and me here, an old maid and a bachelor.'

'Oh, but,' stammered Aggie, who felt she ought to say something to show that Jamie Watson held Auntie Lizzie with more regard than people thought, 'he still kisses her, though! I know, because I—I heard him in the harvest time when I was gathering blackberries along the ditch side.'

There was a moment of astonished silence then Andrew Blackwell gave a shout of laughter.

'That's a good one, Aggie! Next time you go berry-picking I'm coming with you! That's a real good one!'

'Andrew Blackwell, you should be downright affronted!' Miss Blackwell said severely, and Aggie was glad that nobody could see how red her own face was. 'Agnes wasn't meaning it like that at all!'

'Oh, Andrew's just having a little fun,' one of the ladies said soothingly. 'I must say too, that the girls entertained us nicely.'

'Very kind of you, ma'am,' Aggie said behind her mask, and hoped it was the right thing. 'Maybe we'd better get home now.'

'Maybe you will,' Miss Blackwell agreed. 'I know your mother doesn't like you to be away too long,' and she got up to go to the door.

Amid the chorus of 'Goodnights', Aggie turned to take another quick look at the parlour and saw Andrew Blackwell poking the fire and laughing to himself. She was pleased when the cold night air was round her, and John stepped out of the dark shadows where he had been waiting for them.

'I heard you at the Rowan Tree!' he growled at Katy crossly, because he was feeling cold in the frosty air. 'I wish you'd learn something new.'

'Everybody likes it,' she answered calmly, and Aggie heard her beginning to eat an apple.

'John, we've got a lot of apples and nuts and a whole shilling!' Janey's voice chirped. 'Oh, Aggie, where's your hand. It's dark.'

'I'm here, next to you,' Aggie answered, holding on to her sister.

'Would you like an apple from me, John?' Janey then asked.

'I'll get one at home,' he replied more gently. 'Wait and I'll carry you on my back!'

Agnes looked up at the bright and starry sky. She picked out the Plough above the town and followed the milky way until it too got lost in the heavens. All along the east the hills were clear-cut where the moon was about to rise, and the lights of the cottages of the Hillside Village twinkled like more stars.

For once the sight gave her no pleasure for she could not keep her mind off Auntie Lizzie.

It was not fair the way things were, with everybody wondering and talking. Other girls had courted and married long since, and there was Auntie Lizzie with her nice kind ways still being escorted home by Jamie Watson, no further forward than when she was sixteen.

Just then a light blazed across the sky, traced a swift and golden trail and vanished silently into space.

'Oh, look! A shooting star!' Katy cried.

'You have to wish,' said Aggie.

'I wish,' Katy said, standing still in the dark and waiting for John and Janey to go on ahead and not hear. 'I wish it rained on Jamie Watson! And only holy water!'

Aggie, standing with her eyes tight shut, thought it queer that they should both be wishing the same thing.

Chapter Five

T HE bright and lively days of October departed and the sad ones of November crept in. On the anniversary of Armistice Day, there were services in all the churches and the bells tolled with the heavy strokes of a dirge. Mrs McMinn observed the two minutes' silence in the school and as she stood by her desk with her head bowed, Aggie's thoughts turned to Tom Riley, now a big boy, looking forward to leaving school when he would be apprenticed to Jamie Watson. Just now his dark face was grave and old for his years, although he could be as merry and cheeky as the rest at other times.

Da would be standing like that in the furrow and Ma in her kitchen and all the people in the big cities would be so still that you could hear a pin drop as the papers had said last year.

'May the souls of the faithful departed rest in peace. Amen,' said Mrs McMinn in a quiet, even voice, and everybody raised their heads.

The baker's van that had stopped outside the school wall, moved off; somebody on a bicycle, with the bell ringing furiously, rode past; and from the distance came the faint skirl of the bagpipes playing a lament. The school continued its affairs with the quietness still hanging over it.

Every afternoon at half-past three, Mrs McMinn made a sign to Aggie and her sisters to close their books and leave, and they reached home as yet, while it was still daylight.

One day Ma asked Aggie if she would go to Baird, the cloggers up the town, to collect her byre clogs which were in for repair.

'He told Da on Saturday they would be ready tonight for sure. You just have to collect them. I need them, Agnes, otherwise I wouldn't ask you to go,' Ma said. 'And hurry on home after!'

'Mrs Kenny's clogs!' the fat little clogger beamed. 'Come in. I'm just finishing them. I know your Ma needs them, so ten minutes, and they're ready!'

Aggie followed him into his workshop and steered her sisters to the seat along the wall. There was a fine smell of wood and leather and the little lamp on the clogger's bench threw a soft glow round the room. For some time Aggie's interest was taken up with the pairs of wooden soles of all sizes, set along the floor.

'That wee pair would fit me!' Janey whispered.

'I heard you,' the clogger answered. 'And they're far warmer than boots for the winter! It's not far away either, with the nights drawing in quickly enough at that.'

This remark caused Aggie to glance sharply at the small pane of window and to her dismay, she saw that daylight was dwindling. 'Will you be long yet till you're finished, if you please?' she asked.

'Just another minute! There was more to do than I thought,' he replied, hammering away. 'I know you'll want to reach home before darkenin'. There's one ready!'

Moving the two small books and yellow oilskin and sou'-wester out of Janey's bag into her own, she put the clog into the empty bag and slung it over her other shoulder.

'I'll put this one in now, Agnes!' the clogger said, getting up with the second clog. 'Just turn round. There! My, you're loaded like a pack-mule, with two saddle-bags! Now run on home quick, like good lassies!'

'My father will be in on Saturday,' Aggie said shyly on her way out.

'That's all right. The name's good. Just you run on now! Goodnight!'

Out in the street there still remained a hazy daylight but the shop windows were brightly lit.

'We'll have to hurry to get a good length out the road, while it's still clear,' Aggie said. 'Give me your hand, Janey!'

'I wish we lived in the town,' Katy sighed.

'So do I,' agreed Janey. 'Oh, Aggie, did you see the big dolls in that shop? There was one all in blue!'

'Can we not look once at the shoes, Aggie?' Katy begged. 'Just to see if they're still there!'

'I suppose one look will not keep us back that long!' Aggie answered, for she too wanted to look at the shoes that they all dreamed of having. Fine and brown they were, buttoning at the side with one strap and made of leather with just the right shine.

'There they are!' Janey cried, pointing to the shoes in the front right corner. 'Aren't they nice!'

'If we had a pair of these for the school we could get there and back in half the time,' Katy reasoned.

'So we could,' Aggie sighed. 'Maybe Ma will think of it when the pig gets killed. But then Ma will never let us wear them to the school.'

'Huh, and you know Da would cover the soles with tackets and it would be just the same as the boots,' argued Katy.

'Oh, no!' Janey pointed out as they moved away from the window. 'We'd still have the straps.'

Across the bridge one or two lights blinked at their reflections in the water, then came Mrs Gouldie's little shop and after the first bend, which left the town behind, the road lay ahead like a long grey tunnel.

In the distance the outline of the Barrhill and Larg were

just visible but soon they too would disappear in the twilight and then darkness would be at their heels.

They were still on the big road when a man on a bicycle drew up alongside them. 'You're late on the road the night, are ye not?' he asked, getting off and falling into step beside them.

'Yes,' Aggie answered, and wished this stranger would ride on.

'Have you far to go?' he asked.

'No, not very far,' she replied, trying to sound as though home was just a little way ahead.

'Oh, I'm not acquainted with these parts,' said the man. 'Which way does it lie?'

'Just a mile and a half down the road here,' Katy joined in as they crossed to the lane.

'Oh, in that case I'll see you along a bit. Would any of you like a ride on my carrier?'

'No thank you,' Aggie said firmly. 'We'd rather walk.'

'And do ye pass many houses on your way home?' the stranger enquired.

'One or two!' Aggie lied uneasily, but with some instinct of self-protection.

'That's not true, Aggie!' Janey said, looking up at her sister in surprise. 'There's just the Big Farm and it's away past the bend.'

The man chuckled to himself. 'Somebody doesn't tell the truth, eh?' he said. 'Would you like some sweeties?'

'No thank you.'

It came from the three of them for Ma had preached often enough: 'Never take anything from a stranger.'

The high hedge made the lane darker than the Big Road and the walking was more difficult because the surface was rough and uneven. Aggie walked next to the bicycle with the man on the other side of it. She and Katy had Janey by the hand between them and Aggie could feel her little sister's steps were beginning to lag.

Had she been alone, she could have disappeared from the man's sight in the almost dark, for she knew of holes in the hedge and low places in the dike that she could get over with ease, but with Katy and Janey, that was out of the question, and anyway, she was too hampered to run with two full bags over her shoulders. She was beginning to feel very uneasy and helpless.

Several times the man tried to manoeuvre his bike so that he was next to Katy, but Aggie held firmly to Janey's hand and silently managed to keep her place with her two sisters well on the far side.

'I've got some sweets in my pocket. Now if one of you would get on the carrier, I'd run you to your house, and then come back for the other two. Your mother would be awful pleased!'

'My mother doesn't like us to speak to strangers!' Katy burst out. 'She's warned us plenty!'

Aggie trudged silently on. It was nearly dark and she knew that there was little chance of meeting anybody on the lane at this time of day. Folk round about were getting ready to start the milking, or stabling the horses just now. No sound broke the November stillness, just the dry sigh of the bare hawthorn branches on the side of the road.

And always this stranger kept pace with them and sometimes uttered a dreadful little laugh to himself.

'I'll kick him with my big boots!' Aggie said fiercely to herself. 'I'll kick him with the tackety toe-shods on one leg and Katy will kick him with hers on the other if he tries to lay a hand on us. Janey can hide in the whins!'

'I've a pain in my side,' Janey whimpered just then.

'You see!' said the man. 'Here, I'll lift her on to the carrier,' and he stopped on the road.

'Hold tight to my hand and Katy's!' Aggie urged in a voice that trembled slightly as she kept walking on. 'Just hold tight!' and at the same time she wondered how they would pass the darkness of the Little Wood with this unwanted companion.

'There's too much nonsense with you!' the stranger said to Aggie with an angry note in his voice. 'But just you wait!'

68

A real fear now filled Aggie and it took all her courage to keep at Janey's flagging pace. Her legs were moving by themselves and it seemed as though there was not a soul in the whole world but the three of them and this man.

'Aggie!' Katy suddenly said. 'I hear somebody!'

'No, you don't!' the stranger said roughly. 'You're just saying that!'

Aggie tried to listen, and peer into the deep dusk. That dark patch ahead could be the shadow of the Little Wood or the high thorn hedge or the dike or her imagination. And her thumping heart kept her from hearing anything.

'Somebody coughed, 'Katy insisted.

'Aggie, I wish I was home!' Janey sniffed, beginning to be aware of the fear of the other two.

Then the darkness in the distance seemed to come nearer and one dark shadow began to isolate itself from it. There was the soft shuffling of boots walking on the grassy side of the road and a figure emerged from the gloom.

'It's Sandy McLean, the roadman!' cried Aggie in relief. 'Oh, hullo, Sandy!' and she swallowed hard to keep the tears from rising.

'Well, lassies, what's wrong? You're late this night!' the roadmender said. 'Your Ma's fair anxious! She came up to the stables to see if one of the boys would come and meet you. Robert is not far back of me!'

'We were at the cloggers and we had to wait,' Aggie explained, 'and this man with the bike kept coming with us!'

'He's away back!' cried Katy. 'He's not here! Listen!'

All they heard was the click of a pedal turning and growing more faint as the man rode away back into the darkness.

'Did he meddle with ye at all?' asked Sandy sternly.

'He kept offering us sweeties and wanted one of us to ride on his carrier,' Aggie said. 'I was frightened for he went on queer to himself! I was very glad to see you!' and she heaved a deep sigh.

'I'm late getting home tonight,' the roadman explained. 'I stepped into Miss Blackwell's and we got talking. It's just as well too. Come on. I'll go back a bit of the road with you till you meet Robert.'

'Oh, here's Robert!' Janey cried, feeling safe again. 'Sandy, are you not feared to go on to the town by yourself?'

'Not me,' laughed the other. 'I've got two good fists! Mind and tell your father.'

When Robert carried Janey on his back and pretended he was a high-stepping pony, the darkness did not seem so frightening, and even the eerie creaking of the trees in the Little Wood only sounded lonely. But Aggie knew she dare not look behind.

Ma was out in the lane with a lantern in her hand. Aggie could see the glow of light as they came up out of the Rosy Hollow.

'Coo-ee, Ma!' she called out because she knew Ma was worried.

'Oh, my, Agnes, what kept you so late?' she asked as they came forward.

'The clogs weren't ready and we had to wait,' Aggie answered, and then she told her about the stranger.

'I should never have asked you to fetch them!' Ma said, her voice full of annoyance as they all went into the kitchen. 'I'll never do it again. Sit in at the table. I kept you some good potato soup.'

'Did the post bring anything today, Ma? Katy asked as she dipped her bread in the thick soup.

'Oh, just the new catalogue! You can have a look at it after you've done your homework, for it's time I was away to the byre. Keep a good fire on, son, and mind the lamp,' she said to Robert, as she picked up the lantern and went off.

The catalogue! Aggie's spirits soared. The long, dark road, the strange man and her fear, vanished at once, for inside the catalogue were all the things a queen could want —the dresses, the toys, the hats and shoes and the fine china and the furniture. She knew she might safely expect one frock for Sunday out of it when the pig was killed and that would be all, but nothing could stop her from pretending that the pale blue and pink silk party frock and white shoes could be hers too, although the only party she had ever been at was the Christmas party at the school. That did not count as nobody had worn a party frock.

'Janey can look at the catalogue first, eh, Aggie?' Katy said, licking her spoon.

Aggie agreed. She knew that Katy's idea was not entirely due to generosity. Both of them had homework to do and this arrangement allowed Janey to get her 'look' over before the others were ready.

That night, there being no night-school for John, Da got out the bike to go into the town to tell the constable about the stranger.

'He didn't harm ye, but I don't like the sound of him,' he said before he left. 'There are a lot of children going along the country roads from the schools. They have to be protected.'

'Aggie protected us, Da!' Katy spoke up, stumbling a little over the big word. 'She kept the man from coming next to us!'

Da looked at Aggie.

'I'll leave something on the mantelpiece for each of you in the morning,' he said, and he patted her awkwardly on the shoulder.

That was the last of the autumn. The wind swung round to the north, bringing sharp showers of sleet that sprinkled the tops of Cairnsmore and the higher hills with snow. Between the showers a watery sun appeared and the cattle that were huddling against the hedges for shelter came back out again to graze in the open.

On her way to school, bent against the wind, Aggie could see her father in his black oilskins toiling up the furrow behind the plough. She always stopped a moment to see if Meg, the little mare, was in harness with the team. Meg hated the rain and Aggie knew Da would have a lot of coaxing to do when a shower passed over.

The heavy boots no longer bothered the girls for the roads had worn off much of the heaviness and anyway most of the school children wore boots of some kind. Even Eddie Campbell's barefoot days were over, although it was not every day that he wore stockings. He shivered for weeks without a jacket until Ma sent him one of John's that was too small.

Aggie handed the parcel into the teacher's house, where Mr McMinn accepted it without a word and wearing his usual expression of martyrdom. At the morning break Aggie told the teacher about the coat, and like that few people knew where it came from, and Eddie thought it was from Mrs McMinn.

The wind turned to gale force and the rain lashed across the fields in grey sheets that stopped the ploughing.

Ma thought it was too rough to send Janey so Aggie and Katy trudged the road together. It was strange without their little sister plodding behind them, and several times Aggie found herself turning round, forgetting she was not there. They were well clad against the weather with yellow oilskins and sou'westers over their clothes and woollen scarves and gloves that Auntie Lizzie had knitted.

The weather was too bad for Auntie Lizzie to visit— Granda said that anybody who went out in that was worse than daft—and even Cousin John who worked on a farm a few miles on the other side of the town, and who came every Sunday evening on his bike, always with something fresh and interesting to tell, also stayed away.

It was very cosy round the fire in the kitchen in the evening. Aggie noticed that Ma liked it too. The anxious, worried look of the day was gone and she smiled and looked more like the photograph hanging on the wall, that had been taken many years ago on her wedding day.

Da liked to hear the girls say their poetry or hear them read out of their school books. He was fond of poetry, especially the kind that spoke of friends 'far across the sea' or 'the days gone by', and every Sunday night Aggie read out from the local paper the poem that was written by a poetess from Da's own town.

Da was proud of the poetess for she had a different poem in the paper every week.

Then Da went off to his bed, for he was up at half-past four, as he got up first and kindled the fire and put the kettle on. Ma was always last to go to bed, for very often she had mending to do.

One night Aggie, in her gown, came up to the kitchen for a drink of water and there was Ma nodding over a pair of patched trousers before a dying fire.

John never missed the night-school even in the worst weather; Mrs McMinn's advice had given him something to hope for which had steadied his character. He said to Ma that he was quite willing to stay and work on the farm until he was of age to try the police force, and he would go to the night-school every winter till then.

Da said he was learning sense and Aggie wondered if she would ever learn sense too. She wished she could stop being so shy, and know what she wanted to do like John and even Robert, for the latter liked the land and animals just the same as Da, and intended to stay with them.

But Mrs McMinn said that to pass the Qualifying was to open the door to a better future. Aggie sighed as the wind howled in the chimney. She was the oldest of the Kenny girls. She had to try to pass so that the rest would follow.

Later in the night as she lay snuggled in the big bed with Katy and Janey, Aggie listened to the wind swishing through the high hedge and the rain hissing against the window. 'The raging storm' she thought to herself and the words sounded fine with the wind roaring round the house outside and herself inside.

'Aggie!' Janey whispered, after one very strong blast.

'What is it?'

'Do you remember what Mrs McMinn said about the train?'

'What train?'

'The one that went through the hole in the bridge! Supposing the wind blows our bridge away and the night train doesn't know!'

'That was long ago when the bridges weren't so strong.'

'Oh!' Janey paused. 'Aggie!'

'What is it now?'

'Supposing the house is lifted up in the air!'

'It can't!' whispered Aggie in return. 'It's built too deep into the ground. You'd better get to sleep, Janey!'

'If we go up into the air, it will be like in an aeroplane,' Katy laughed softly.

'There you go with your aeroplanes!' Aggie said, leaning up on her elbow. 'Everybody knows that aeroplanes will never come to anything,' she added as much to herself as to her sister. Several times she had seen an aeroplane flying through the clouds, a tiny speck that droned and hummed for a long time after it was out of sight.

'Nathan Thomson says that man must not dare God too much,' she said again.

'John says that they'll get bigger and bigger and carry folks like boats in the sky,' persisted Katy. 'He saw it in the paper. And I'll go to America in one when I'm big!'

'Maybe you'll fall out!' said Janey hoarsely, 'and you'll wish you had stayed in the train.'

'Sh! There's Ma!' warned Katy.

Aggie heard Ma's slippered feet scuffling along the passage to their room. She often wondered how she could hear them above the storm outside, but she always did.

'Are you all right, Agnes?' she asked, pushing the door open and letting the candlelight flicker in.

'Yes, Ma.'

'Try and sleep then, and Katy and Janey too. The wind will be gone in the morning.'

Aggie shut her eyes with determination while Katy and

Janey settled down again. Her mind went to the aeroplanes and the tales that Katy wove about them. She had no liking for such fancies. The ride in the doctor's car had been a great thing but she still would rather sit on the spring-cart behind Prince, the black, high-stepping pony that Abie Irvine of the Home Farm lent to Da every year to take them to the Cattle Show. Da just sat there with the reins in his hand, Ma beside him and the three girls at his back, murmuring a word here and there and leisurely looking at the fields rolling by on either side. 'I don't think the doctor lifted his eyes off the road once!' she muttered to herself, 'and what a lot of wheels and handles.'

As she drifted off to sleep she heard Robert go out with the lantern to see if the hens and pig were well shut in, as he had done every night since he left the school.

Chapter Six

NEXT morning the wind had dropped and a glimmer of sun appeared from behind Cairnsmore-of-Fleet. Pools of water lay on the fields and from the door Aggie could hear the deep flow of the river which would be swirling in spate and sucking at the sandbanks after all the rain.

Ma's face was grave and her voice anxious. 'I'm awfully annoyed!' she told Aggie as she dished up the breakfast. 'Last night when Robert went out to the pig, he was lying on his side and his meat was still in his trough. He hadn't touched it. This morning it's just the same!'

Aggie was at a loss for an answer. She was fond of Henry and she often thought he lived a lonely life with a sad end. In a matter of weeks now he would be slaughtered and sold and they would all get the things they needed with the money. It was a terrible thing and every year it was the same. You loved the pig and then one day, always in the back end of the year, you came home from school to a blank silence and you had a lump in your throat for days.

Ma never said when the pig-killer was coming, for she knew how the girls all felt about Henry.

'What does Da say?' Aggie asked.

'He's bringing Andrew Blackwell down to see him. Maybe he can give him a dose of something,' Ma replied, sighing as she added: 'There's that much needed! Come on, Janey, it's time you were getting into your coat.'

'Oh, Mr Blackwell will do something, Ma!' Aggie answered with relief in her voice. 'You remember when the Marley cow got into the clover? He helped her then. I'll run and see Henry before I leave for the school!'

The pig was lying on his side in the straw, his small eyes half-shut and his great sides heaving and panting.

'Henry! Oh, Henry!' Aggie said with tears in her eyes. 'Are you sick, Henry?'

The pig made a short sound between a squeal and a grunt and his eyes blinked in recognition.

'Henry, if you don't get better it will be hard on Ma, and if you do get better it's the worse for you! Oh, I don't know what to say!'

She gave a gulp as she turned away and took the long way round the garden so that her eyes would have lost their redness when Katy saw her.

It was one of the longest days at school that Aggie could remember, for all the time the vision of the pig lying panting helplessly in his sty came between her and her books. Mrs McMinn seemed to sense her preoccupation, for she was after her the whole day.

'Agnes Kenny, dreaming again! That will certainly help you to pass the Qualifying! Come out to my desk!'

'I would stick up for you, Aggie, if I could!' Eddie Campbell sympathized with her later, for his heart was big. 'But I would only get two on each hand and I have chilblains,' and he showed her his swollen knuckles.

'Oh, never mind, Eddie, I keep thinking about Henry! He's very sick.'

'Henry! Henry who?' Eddie asked in surprise, for he thought he knew all the Kennys there were to know.

'Oh, just Henry! He's somebody we're acquainted with at home,' she replied, moving away, for how could you explain

77

to anybody that you loved your pig the way some folk loved their dogs.

They hurried home faster than usual that night although they never lingered at all since the incident with the stranger. For the first time Aggie realized what Ma meant when she gave her warnings every day when they left for school. She had avoided strangers before mainly because she was shy, but now she knew they were to be feared and all three of them were glad to leave the Big Road at night and turn into the lane for that was where they were likeliest to meet the folk they knew.

But this night, as soon as they had passed Miss Blackwell's Farm and come up out of Rosy Hollow, which was now a tangle of bare briars, they strained their ears for the grunts and squeals from the pig sty.

There was a stony silence.

'Henry!' Katy called out cautiously, for she had less patience than the other two.

There was no answer and when Aggie saw Ma's strained face at the door, she knew everything was wrong.

The pig was dead.

The gloom that lay on the Kennys that night reminded Aggie of the other times when the cloud of melancholy had hovered over the house, for like the rest of the world the people in the Little Valley had their days of sorrow as well as of joy.

She remembered the loss of the small brother, so many years ago now, that it appeared like a dream. Then there had been the fire in the stables at the Home Farm with all the horses inside, and then Wallie Johnstone's young brother, Jimmy, was killed in action and the folk in the Valley could hardly believe it, because it seemed no time since he left the school. Along the lane near the Little Wood, Mr Williams of the bank had died against the dike-side, when out for his Sunday walk. Someone had grooved a cross into the stone of the dike to mark the spot where death had lurked that bright day.

But the saddest of all was the spring of a year or two back when the Big Flu was sweeping the land and Roderick McClurg's two daughters were both taken in one week.

Aggie would never forget Bessie and Mary McClurg as long as she lived for they had visited the house ever since she could remember and it was queer when they suddenly stopped coming.

Roderick had wept openly on Ma's kitchen table and Ma had patted his back to console him, her own tears streaming down her face. After that Aggie heard it said that the McClurgs were not getting over the loss of their girls.

'Hiding themselves from folks and burying themselves in sorrow!' Nathan Thomson said. 'It does no good.'

One Sunday night Aggie and her sisters were taking a walk down the lane along with Ma, not hurrying, just sauntering along in the warm sunlight of the June evening.

Suddenly the notes of a bugle rang out from the Hill-top, distant yet clear, slow and full of splendour.

They all stood and listened and Janey asked urgently: 'What is it, Ma?'

'Sh!' said Ma softly. 'It's a hymn they're playing. That's "Lead Kindly Light".'

'I think it's the Angel Gabriel!' said Katy in a tense whisper, for she had been hearing of the Last Day from Mrs McMinn.

The notes rang out over the Little Valley now faint, now clear, but full of such pleading that Aggie, young as she was, stood entranced and wished it would go on and on. The music died away and there was no more of it.

'Nobody knows who he was,' Nathan Thomson told them all not long after, when he was along at the house. 'He was a stranger, and nobody saw him climb the brae face to the hilltop either! And he went back the way he came! My, that bugle threw a fine echo round the hills, and everybody in the Hill Village and the Little Valley came out to listen! And Roderick McClurg and the wife as well! And you know what else they say?'

'No!'

'That since then the McClurgs are changed folks, they have found peace in their hearts. Aye, an' fresh courage, too!' and Nathan rolled out the words in his rich tones.

'Ah, poor souls!' Ma said with great sympathy. 'I sincerely hope it is so!' And there was a small silence after her words.

All these things passed through Aggie's mind as she looked round the silent supper table, and she wished too that something would happen to the Kennys that would take them all back to last week when everything was fine. As she bit into a piece of scone she wondered how she was going to keep back the tears that were about to rise, and she tried hard to think of something that was merry and gay.

She was just going over Mamie Ross's wedding at the Home Farm cottage last year with the singing and dancing and fun when Andrew Blackwell arrived with the vet. The lanterns were lit and they all trooped outside, including Ma, leaving Aggie to look after her sisters and see to the fire. Then she heard the rain begin to fall, softly and gently from the bay, and Ma came back in, her oilskins dripping water, and raindrops streaming down the lantern.

'The rain isn't heavy, but it's thick,' she said, blowing out the light and setting the lantern back on its shelf in the lobby; then she sat down on Da's high-backed chair at the fireside. She stared silently into the fire for a moment and Aggie saw the raindrops glistening on the strands of dark hair round her face in the firelight. She looked very sad.

'What did the man say, Ma?' Katy asked.

Ma raised her head and looked at them. 'Well, I must tell you that things will not be the same this year as last year!' she said in a flat kind of voice. 'I had hoped to buy the clothes that were needed, and some new bedding and put a little by, but it was not meant to be. And of course, you'll not be getting any Sunday frocks either!'

'Ma, we don't care, do we, Aggie?' Katy answered quickly,

going over to her mother, and Aggie wished she could do and say all these things as readily as Katy. 'We never think of Sunday frocks!'

'No, Ma. Truly we don't. We're sorry about the pig but we don't care about the frocks! My kilt's good enough anyway.' Aggie agreed, her emotion drawing the words from her 'And we'll get another pig again,' and she took her mother's sou'wester and hung it up.

'Henry's in heaven, Ma!' Janey assured her.

Ma smiled a little. 'There will not be another pig for a wee while. The vet says we've got to pull down the pighouse and burn it all up and not keep a pig till we've built a new sty in another place,' Ma explained, and added: 'We never had this happen since we got married nearly twenty years ago, your Da and me.' She sighed again, and said: 'All that will take time and money!'

'Robert and John will help to build it, Ma,' Aggie said. 'Will I make you a cup of tea?'

'There's nothing I'd like better, Agnes. However, if we all keep well, it's the main thing! But I'm sorry about your new frocks.' She paused and looked at them again. 'Janey, you're dead tired. Come, I'll put you to bed while Agnes gets the cups out.'

'We can pretend about the Sunday frocks like we do about the strap shoes, Ma,' Aggie heard Janey say as she went along the passage to the bedroom.

The gloom lasted several days and then gradually lifted, for, as Ma said, as long as they were all in good health that was the main thing. Jamie Watson, out to meet Auntie Lizzie on her next visit, offered straight away to help build the pig-house, and knew where he could get planks quite cheap to start off with.

Roderick McClurg and Nathan Thomson came to sympathize, and the former, waggling his long moustache, said his sow would have a litter soon and by the time February was in, Da could have his pick. Nathan Thomson never had anything to give, for he and his family lived for the day, but his deep voice was very soothing, and Aggie could have listened to him all night.

So the old pig-house was taken apart and burned one Sunday afternoon and Cousin John came out to give Da a hand. Sunday was the only day there was time, for it was dark before the day's work was over during the week.

'The boys are away to Tony Griffin's over at the Village,' Da explained. 'They potter about in his big shed.'

'Oh, they have to get away sometimes,' Cousin John said as he leaned his bike against the fence. 'There's not much amusement for young ones away out here.'

Cousin John was many years older than either Robert or John and he talked to Da as one man to another.

Aggie and Katy stood at a distance and watched them pile the planks on top of some dry straw soaked in paraffin. When Da threw a lighted match on to the heap, there was a great blaze.

'You know,' Cousin John called out to Da amid the crackling of the flames, 'there's talk of us on the farms getting the half-day on a Saturday!'

Da's face lit up with interest.

'You don't say!' he said.

'Aye!' continued Cousin John, leaning his long figure on a graip. 'In fact the time will come when everybody will get a half-day in the week not counting the Sunday, of course.'

'Well, I for one would like it,' Da replied, straightening his back for a minute. 'Although I can't complain. Andrew Blackwell lets us all home on a Saturday by four o'clock. Mind ye, there's a lot of odd jobs I could do on a Saturday afternoon. But maybe that's all just a lot of talk!' and he went back to throwing the old planks on to the red ashes.

'Time will tell,' said Cousin John, 'but there's many a man like myself who has to work till six on the Saturday like any other day, and grooms and feeds horses on the Sunday forbye! The week never ends for me!'

Suddenly Da called out. 'Agnes, chase those hens away from the fire!'

Aggie grabbed a stick and swirling it in the air, rushed among the white hens, whose curiosity had brought them too close. With a chorus of cackles they fled hastily back down the field, their feet barely touching the ground, with Aggie running behind them.

'Bah!' she panted to the big white cockerel when they reached the hen-house. 'It should have been you, not Henry!' but she quickly got out of his way before he thought of answering back.

Shortly after that Da scattered the last of the grey ashes and marked off the place where the new pig-house would stand. 'That's the best we can do now,' he remarked. 'There's more rain coming. That'll smother any redness that's left. I think we'll go in.'

The rain fell soft and thick, lasting several days, and everybody said it was mild for the time of year, for December was just in. Then late one afternoon the sky cleared in the west and there was the sharp curved blade of a moon just above Barrhill.

'The new moon!' cried Katy, for on these short days dusk was falling before they arrived home. 'We should turn our money.'

'We haven't got any!' Aggie said, stopping to look. 'That will be the Christmas moon. I think she's a frosty one.'

'How do you know, Aggie?' Janey enquired.

'Because the moon is not on her back. Da says we're due for a change of weather,' Aggie answered.

With the waxing of the moon the rainy mists disappeared and the hills stood blue and cold. In the morning a sift of rime lay on the roadside grass and thin skins of ice covered the puddles. From behind Cairnsmore the sun rose in a great golden light that dimmed as he travelled above the bay to the west. He set in a crimson haze as the moon flooded the Little Valley with a pale glow and silvered the fields with frost.

In the town the shops were decorated with holly for Christmas and New Year. Sometimes the three girls had time in the dinner-hour to go up the street and look in the shop windows. The sleeping dolls, the fat annuals, the cakes covered with fancy icing, the boxes of shortbread, and chocolate and crystallized fruits, and the pink sugar mice, that filled the windows, tempted them to stare long enough but they always kept a spare minute to look at the shoes.

Never did they linger near the butcher's, for there was generally a pig's head on display, with an orange in its open mouth, and Henry was still a painful memory.

In the school there was an undertone of excitement, for the Christmas holidays were drawing near. One day, Mrs McMinn after going over the story of Bethlehem and the meaning of the Christmas spirit, made an announcement.

'Attention everyone!'

There was immediate silence.

'On the day the school closes next week, there will be a Christmas party with a Christmas tree, held here in the school, and given to you by members of the congregation.

'A great lady of the district has been generous enough to remember you and everybody will receive a present. I hope you all come neatly and tidily dressed, with well-scrubbed hands and faces.'

She stopped and there was a buzz of excited whispers. Every year this happened and the thrill was always tremendous. Last year Aggie had received *The Last of the Mohicans* and she was already hoping that she would get a book again this year. Once again Mrs McMinn interrupted her thoughts and the cane rattled sharply on the desk in front of her.

'Come along now, Agnes! You have two whole weeks over Christmas and New Year in which you can do nothing except, of course, the homework I intend to give you.'

Aggie bent her head again and thought the Christmas spirit was sadly lacking in the teacher.

Nevertheless, the signs of the holy season were everywhere. On the mantelpiece at home stood the Christmas cards sent by uncles and aunts from other places, some far away like

Da's sister in Canada. More would come as the New Year drew nearer for in the south-west Christmas was a feast of the church and of the children whose parents could afford it. New Year was for everybody.

On the Sunday before Christmas a crib with the Child Jesus in life size stood in the church. Janey was not there to see it as Da thought she should stay at home with him because of the hard frost. It was freezing cold in the church and Aggie, sitting between Ma and Robert, with John at the other side of Ma, wondered what it was like in the choir where Katy was.

Katy had never been in the choir before but Mrs McMinn, who played the organ, had asked her to sing 'Silent Night' during the Christmas season.

'In praise of the Holy Child, Katherine,' she had insisted gently when she saw Katy hesitate.

'Yes, ma'am,' Katy had agreed. 'I'll go this Sunday.'

There was a lot of coughing and sneezing and shuffling about in the church, for everybody was cold. Only Grandma and Granda, sitting with Auntie Lizzie in the seat in front of Aggie, hardly moved. They kept their eyes on their prayer books, Grandma a firm little figure in a heavy black cloth coat, and Granda in a loose tweed cape with holes for his arms, because he said overcoats were new-fangled.

Aggie stole a look at Auntie Lizzie and saw her lips were moving.

'I expect she's praying for Jamie's christening!' she thought, and decided that she would pray for that too.

Soon however, she began to feel cold, first her fingers inside the woollen gloves, then her toes went numb. She tried to curl them up inside the button boots to warm them but more and more it was like standing with her feet in cold water. She knew she ought to try to say some prayers as Ma said there was plenty to pray for, but her cold hands and feet were taking up all her attention.

Then she remembered the two rabbits that were cooking in the big black pot on the side of the fire at home. She could almost smell them in the thick brown onion gravy. Two rabbits, she thought. That would be eight legs and there were seven Kennys! Oh, she would certainly get a front leg anyway!

The organ started to play very softly and she remembered where she was with a quick feeling of shame. If people only knew what she was thinking! She hoped it didn't show on her face.

Then Katy began to sing.

'Silent night, holy night . . .'

At first Aggie heard just a little nervous tremble in her sister's voice, then it went away and the notes came pure and clear. The coughing and the sneezing stopped, and everybody was listening. They were listening so intently that there was not a breath of sound but Katy's young voice, and the soft notes of the organ in the still, cold church.

Aggie listened too, for the feeling of Christmas was creeping in and all round. It made her forget the cold and believe that the Star of Bethlehem could be shining overhead even here in the Little Valley.

When the church came out, several people praised Katy's singing to Ma, who cleared her throat with nervous pride.

'Such a voice must not be wasted, Mrs Kenny!' one lady urged her. 'You really should do something about it.'

'What can I do about it?' Ma said sadly, when they were all on the Big Road. 'I don't know anything of these things. You need learnin' for all that.'

'But Ma, Mrs McMinn gives me singing lessons every day,' Katy answered, sliding on the hard ice that now covered the puddles.

'I don't know how Mrs McMinn manages the time for all these things,' was Ma's only comment as they trudged on in the cold sunlight.

At last it was the closing day for the school holidays and the day of the Christmas party.

When Ma saw Aggie and her sisters off that morning, she was full of reminders about their manners.

'Now don't forget to say "if you please" or "thank you" or "beg pardon" as is needful!'

'No, Ma.'

'And no sliding in your Sunday boots!'

'No, Ma.'

'And put on your gloves and mufflers at playtime.'

'Aggie!' Janey asked along the lane, 'what for do you say "beg pardon"?'

'That's for the hiccups!' Katy replied quickly. 'Did ye not know that?'

'No.' Then again in a voice that quavered a little. 'Aggie, I'm cold.'

It was cold, with the frost thick and white on everything and a little icy breath of wind coming from the east, where the sun's early rays were struggling through the frosty mist.

'Give me your hand, Janey,' Aggie said, turning round, 'you'll get warmer as you keep walking!'

'And wait till you see the Christmas tree!' Katy promised. 'You'll not think of the cold.'

When they reached the school and hung up their coats in the porch, they tiptoed into the next room, which was partitioned off the schoolroom.

'Oh!' said Janey, with a long breath of pleasure, 'there it is!'

In one corner stood the Christmas tree. The three of them stopped and stared at it, for they only saw one once a year and this was the second in Janey's life.

'Aggie, it's got candles on it!' she whispered.

'And silver bells and coloured things!' said Katy. 'Oh, Aggie, do you see the star at the top?'

Aggie nodded.

'It goes up to the ceiling,' she whispered back.

Just then the schoolroom door opened and Mrs McMinn appeared. Aggie turned quickly, expecting the worst.

'Come along in, girls,' the teacher smiled sweetly. 'You may look at the tree later if you promise not to touch it.'

'Yes, ma'am,' Aggie answered in a surprised daze, and

she saw the teacher was wearing her best navy costume with the braid trimming. She knew then that the holidays had started.

If all the school days had been like that one, nobody would have cared if they got a free Saturday or not. After prayers there were warming-up exercises with the piano, tidying of desks and cleaning of inkwells, and the telling of stories. Then Mrs McMinn took the Qualifying Class and gave them notes of the work she hoped they would do in the holidays.

'It will keep you occupied on those days you can't go out, because of bad weather,' she beamed, 'besides helping you on with your schoolwork,' and Aggie felt no resentment at all at being given homework to do during the holidays.

In no time the morning was over and the teacher was telling them all that the party would start at three o'clock.

'Perhaps the older boys would be kind enough to stack the desks away just now so that the ladies have plenty of room for the preparations.'

'Yes, ma'am!' Eddie Campbell, Bernard Jones, Tom Riley and his brother all answered in one voice, and they set to with a great deal of noise as the rest of the school left.

The girls wore their best pink woollen jumpers that Auntie Lizzie had knitted, over their school skirts, since they had no other.

'Don't eat too much!' Granda kept yelling at them. 'Pastries are the ruination of the country!'

'Pastries once a year will not kill anybody,' Grandma said. 'Enjoy yourselves the three of you!'

The December sun was already sinking behind the trees in the Park Wood and the frost was chilling the air when Aggie reached the school yard. Round the porch the rest of the children were all clustered, chattering with the excitement of the joys to come. Beneath Cathie Gemmell's coat, Aggie caught a glimpse of brown velvet. Her heart sank a little for the Sunday frocks that Ma had picked for them out of the catalogue, were trimmed with brown velvet.

Just then the bell rang and Eddie Campbell, who had offered his services inside, appeared at the porch door. At first Aggie hardly recognized him for he wore a new navy jersey and trousers, his face was shining with much scrubbing, and his fair hair was slicked and plastered down.

'You can all come in now,' he said loudly, with an air of great importance. 'And no pushing!'

'Don't you tell us what to do, Eddie Campbell!' Helen McKay snapped. 'You're not the teacher.'

'It's just as well for you!' he replied, poking out his tongue at her as she pushed past him.

As Aggie walked into the porch, Eddie shoved his head under her nose.

'Smell!' he ordered.

Aggie stopped and sniffed.

'Scented soap!' he informed her proudly. 'My Granny got it for the party!'

Inside the schoolroom, many changes had taken place since the forenoon.

The partitions had been taken down and there was one big room where there were two before. The desks had been piled up at the far end and benches were placed down both sides of a long, white-covered table. A wide space was left in the middle of the room for party games.

Everybody's eyes were on the Christmas tree, and Aggie wished Ma could have seen it for she had never seen one in her life except on a Christmas card. All its candles were alight, casting a warm glow in the wintry dimness of the schoolroom. On its branches little parcels wrapped in coloured paper were hanging, and other parcels were lying round the foot.

'Come along in, children,' Mrs McMinn called out as she moved away from a group of ladies busy at a table near the stove. 'We'll start off with some games. Bernard Jones, as you're the tallest, will you please light the gas? Now, do you all know musical chairs?'

They played all the games that were played other years—

'Blind man's Buff', 'I sent a Letter to my Love' and 'Hunt-the-slipper' with the little hand-bell from Mrs McMinn's desk in place of a slipper; it was more fun to find, as a tinkle gave it away. In between, Cathie Gemmell played the piano, the McKay sisters recited a poem for two people, and others, including Katy, sang songs with actions.

As Aggie looked round at all the laughing faces, she felt relieved that so far Mrs McMinn, in her search for performers, had passed her by, for this was no day for 'Mary, go and call the cattle home.' It was far too sad.

Then the ladies called out that tea was ready and they all sat down on the benches at the long table, trying not to appear too eager.

While Mrs McMinn was saying grace, Aggie managed to open one eye to take a look at all the good things on the table, remembering to keep the eye next to the teacher tight shut.

That morning along the road Aggie had warned Katy and Janey to watch out and not make the mistake she had made at last year's Christmas party. She had been very hungry and had taken a big half of buttered scone which had been a struggle to get completely through, and she never tasted one of the little three-cornered sandwiches or pastries that Granda raved so much against.

This year things were going better, for the sandwiches were passed along first and when the scones were handed round she took a small one. Just then Mrs McMinn came behind her with the teapot and poured some into her cup.

'Have a good tea, Agnes,' she said in a low voice. 'You have a long walk home, and it's a cold night! I'll bring the scones along again.'

'Yes, ma'am,' answered Aggie, and remembered to add hastily, 'if you please, ma'am.' And there again two scones sat side by side on her plate, much the same as the big one of last year.

Perhaps it was because she was a year older, but she

managed to get through them both without any trouble and still have room for the cakes that followed.

Taking one that was piled high with coconut, she looked down the table at Janey who was holding up a little pink cake in a paper case. 'Look, Aggie! Pink icing!' she was saying. 'Pink icing!'

Aggie nodded and smiled and then looked at Katy who had a daub of red on her cheek from a jelly tart. Satisfied that her sisters were missing nothing, she bit into her own with the greatest satisfaction.

'That was a grand feed, Aggie!' Eddie Campbell said later when they were all leaving the table. 'I lost count of the sandwiches and cakes I had,' and he wiped his hands vigorously on the seat of his trousers.

'It's not finished yet,' Helen McKay said. 'We have to get the presents from the Christmas tree!'

After the bigger ones had taken the little ones out for a moment, they all sat in a half-circle round the tree. There was a few minutes earnest discussion between Mrs McMinn and the ladies, during which Aggie tried to guess what the parcels contained by the shape of them, and the whispering round her told her that the rest of the school was doing the same. Then the teacher announced that one of the ladies had kindly consented to present the gifts and as the lady came forward with a pleasant smile, everybody clapped loudly.

At first there was silence as the parcels were taken from the tree one by one and handed to their owners, then murmurs of approval when they were opened, that developed into loud exclamations.

'Look! I've got a box of paints!'

'Oh, isn't she nice! Real hair, too!'

'Aggie!' Katy called out, 'I've got a sewing-set! And a thimble! And thread in all the colours!'

'Rose Riley's got a tea-set,' somebody said.

Agnes Kenny. That was her name. She got up and thanked the lady as she received the hard, square parcel. It was a book; she could feel it as she opened it excitedly. *Ivanhoe* by Sir Walter Scott. One she had not yet read.

'I got *Little Women*' whispered Cathie Gemmell. 'We can change over later on!'

Mary Jane Kenny. That was Janey, and Aggie watched as her little sister took the long box and Mrs McMinn helped her with the string and the paper. The lid was lifted and Janey's face was pale as she drew out the flaxen haired doll in the blue dress. She held it up for a minute, fingered the frock, then raised the skirt a little. A sigh of satisfaction escaped her, for it was complete, the lace-edged knickers were there too. She looked round to Aggie with a wide smile of bliss lighting up her face.

Then the party was over. Mrs McMinn asked them all to thank the ladies for everything, which they did wholeheartedly. Then the lady who had presided at the Christmas tree asked them to thank Mrs McMinn for all that she had done. They cheered loudly, for the teacher in the holidays was quite different from the teacher in school-time, just as they themselves were.

Before they left Mrs McMinn made a quiet little speech in which she wished them all a Happy and a Holy Christmas and New Year.

'The school reopens,' she concluded, 'on the sixth day of January at nine o'clock sharp. For the country ones it will be nine-thirty.'

As Aggie scrambled into the porch with the others for her coat, she saw Robert who had come to meet them, waiting at the school door.

'Button up your coats well,' he said to Aggie. 'It's the hardest frost yet!'

As she helped her sisters into their things, she heard him stamping his feet up and down the yard and she supposed he had been waiting some time in the cold. She shivered herself in the frosty air, for it had been warm in the school-room.

On the way out the Big Road, when Katy and Janey were

telling Robert about the party and the Christmas tree, Aggie looked up at the night sky. It was Christmas Eve and a full moon was rising above Cairnsmore. Big white clouds were piling up above the hills in the north-east and now and again there was a drift across the face of the moon.

Tonight she and her sisters would hang up their stockings over the end of the big bed and before Ma went out to the byre in the morning she would slip an apple and an orange and something like a ball or a skipping-rope into them, for their Christmas. Otherwise Christmas Day was like any other day, with the shops in the town open and everybody doing their day's work.

As they left the Big Road and went into the lane, Aggie remembered that it was here on the first day of school that Katy and Janey had stripped off their boots and stockings because of the heat. And Katy had said it would soon be the Christmas holidays. At that time they had seemed a long way off, and yet they were here now.

Chapter Seven

THE clouds that rose up behind the hills on Christmas Eve carried snow, and showers of fine stinging sleet swept down into the Little Valley. Cairnsmore and the hills to the north were dazzling white but the frost at night shrunk the snow in the low-lying fields to hard icy patches.

'It's a good thing you have your holidays just now,' Ma said, looking out over the wintry landscape. 'You are better at home this cold weather. It's enough to get a fever.'

'And you're on your holidays too, Ma!' Janey laughed.

As it was calving time and the cows were going dry, Ma had stopped milking just after Christmas and would not be going to the byre for several weeks. Miss Blackwell and her brother were going to manage by themselves during that time.

Aggie thought it was fine with Ma at home, especially when she got up in the morning and heard her moving about in the kitchen, instead of just the lonely tick-tock of the clock on the dresser. Since Ma no longer went to the milking Aggie went up to the farmhouse at first daylight to fetch the milk. In the west, a lop-sided moon was fading to pale gold and here and there a prick of light from a late star pierced the blue blanket of the sky.

THE COUNTRY ONES

Aggie dallied up the lane where the cart-tracks were hard as iron and the ice made dark mirrors in the ruts. She went slowly because she liked being alone to watch the sun's rays appear over the edge of Cairnsmore.

'Soon there will be no days left!' she mumbled to herself, standing still to watch the sunrise although she was shivering. 'Mrs McMinn says the world goes round, I wonder if it slows down on the last week of the year!'

When the sun rose in the south-west on a winter's morning, the colours were unbelievable. The sky in the east was painted with all shades of yellow, rose and deepest orange, that vanished into mist as the new day filled the valley.

'I'd better hurry now,' Aggie thought, after seeing the sun safely on his journey, 'or Ma will wonder if I've spilled the milk or something.'

Miss Blackwell filled the milk-can and remarked on the cold. 'The pumps are all frozen,' she grumbled, 'and that makes a lot of extra work!'

'Da covered our pump with bags,' Aggie answered. 'It looks just like—like somebody standing there!'

'I expect it will!' Miss Blackwell laughed plumply, 'but I always complain in cold weather. I just don't like it. I never get far out in the summer, but I always feel I'm shut right away from everything in the winter. Oh well!' she shrugged her broad shoulders. 'In a day or two it will be New Year. How's your Ma liking her rest from the byre?'

'Oh, she's liking it fine,' answered Aggie, thinking that everybody else liked it too.

'Tell her Betsy and Tilda calved last night. Andrew got up and went out to them. It's my turn to-night and I hope it thaws before then,' Miss Blackwell told her, 'but I don't suppose it will.'

There was no sign of a thaw and the wind stayed in the east, a cold and freezing breath, that glued the rime to the dead leaves and withered grass on the roadsides. The ground was too hard for ploughing so Da mended harness in the stable and took the horses in to the blacksmith's in the town.

Robert and John carted turnips and fodder to the beasts that were still outside.

Ma was getting the house ready for the New Year and there was a great smell of baking and home-made ginger wine. On Hogmanay two hens were killed, one for the next day's breakfast and the other for Grandma and Granda Breen. Aggie knew that Ma took this very badly for she felt for her hens the same way the girls felt about the pig.

That night Da and the boys went into the town with Grandma's hen, a pair of rabbits for Mrs Riley and some fresh eggs and potato scones for Mrs McMinn. When they returned, Da produced the New Year bottle of whisky from his inside pocket, and laid it reverently on the dresser, well to the back so that nobody could knock it over.

All through the year Da saved and scraped to buy the bottle of whisky, for to him it was a matter of pride. He managed to gather the money together from what he made on market days, or harvesting at other farms, or when the threshing mill came round, for every Saturday he left his wage on the corner of the mantelpiece for Ma to pick up—every penny of it—as Aggie had heard her say to Auntie Lizzie many times.

'I had a dram from your father,' he said to Ma, as he hung up his ulster behind the door. 'They were very pleased with the hen.'

'There's some stir in the town tonight, I can tell you!' John announced, holding his hands out to the fire. 'There's going to be a tar-barrel procession!'

'And the pipe band's out as well,' said Robert. 'I saw them gathering at the square, when I took the rabbits to Mrs Riley.'

'Were there many folk about?' Ma inquired.

'Not that many,' Da replied. 'It's not like it was before the war, although I saw plenty the worse of drink.'

'I would like to have seen the procession,' John said.

'Oh, it will not be on till near midnight!' Da answered, drawing his big wooden chair closer to the fire. 'I'm right glad to get back home. The sky's bonny with stars, but I think it's freezing harder than ever!'

Aggie listened to all this with interest for she was keeping as wide awake as possible, since she was going to sit up with Ma and Da and her brothers until the clock struck midnight and the New Year was there. What happened then was something she had always wondered about. Once Nathan Thomson had said that if you looked out of the door when the clock was striking you never knew what you might see. The idea was too horrifying to think about.

Last year Aggie had started off to see the old year out, but she had become so sleepy that she had to go to bed long before the time. Tonight, being a year older, it was going to be different, and as she sat on the little stool by the fire, with one of the cats curled up on the cloth mat between her feet, and listened to the talk of the others, she felt she could stay up the whole night long. The fire hissed and crackled and sent sparks up the chimney, the kettle dirled on the hob, and Aggie's head began to nod. Quickly she straightened up. It was a long way off midnight yet. A few minutes later her head nodded and she lurched forward.

'Agnes,' she heard Ma say, 'you're better in your bed. You'll fall in the fire!'

'Oh no, Ma,' she mumbled, trying to keep her eyes open. 'I'm wide awake!'

'With both eyes shut,' John snickered.

'Your ma's right,' Da said. 'You're better lying down. Anyway it's the New Year the whole day tomorrow!'

Aggie got up and went, bleary-eyed, along the passage to the bedroom, not daring to glance at the front door, with all the night on the other side of it, as she passed by. She heard the night train come down the line, sounding very near in the frost, and its whistle seemed to mock her as she got into bed. She would have to wait another year before she found out the secret of the passing of the old year and the coming in of the new one.

It was a strange thing to wake up on New Year's morning

and know it was another year—'a brand new year'—as Ma said when she pulled up the blind in the half-dark, 'with everything white with frost.'

'I'd like you to get up now, the three of you!' she told them. 'Da and the boys are up at the stables feeding the horses, and they'll bring the milk down with them. They'll expect to see the breakfast on the table when they come back as they just had a drink of tea before they left. They'll not be working the next two days, except for doing the horses and the beasts!'

Aggie got up and dressed quickly and then collected Katy's and Janey's clothes. 'I'll take them to the kitchen!' she told them. 'If you run quickly along the passage in your gowns, you'll not feel the cold!'

A big fire burned in the grate and the kitchen was full of the smell of boiling fowl.

Ma had covered the oilcloth on the table with a white table cloth and Aggie got out the willow pattern cups and saucers.

'You have to smile all day today!' Katy remarked as she dragged her jumper over her head, 'because then you'll smile for all the rest of the year!'

'Katy, you'd better not smile all the time at Mrs McMinn or you'll get the cane!' Janey said very seriously.

'I'll likely get the cane anyway,' replied her sister brightly, determined to keep her good humour.

Just then Da and the boys came in, champing their feet and blowing their hands, and presently they were all taking their places round the table—all except Da.

Going over to the dresser he poured out six glasses of ginger wine from one bottle and a small glass of whisky from the other bottle.

'Will you have a wee dram?' he asked Ma before he set the bottle down.

'No thanks, maybe later,' Ma replied. 'A glass of ginger wine will do nicely.'

The glasses were handed round and Da went back to his

place at the table. Looking at them all very gravely he raised the glass of whisky first to Ma and then to the rest of the family.

'A Happy New Year to you all!' he said.

'The same to you!' they all echoed and as Aggie swallowed her drink, she noticed for the first time that both Robert and John were taller than Da—a good deal taller; in fact they were leaving Da well behind.

'That's queer,' she puzzled to herself. 'I thought Da was a big man.' Her eyes slid round to Katy but all she could see was her pink tongue poking down to the bottom of the wineglass.

There was boiled fowl for the breakfast with scones and butter and slices of a long spicy fruit loaf which Katy had measured and found to be eighteen inches long. The hen was eaten at this meal because by dinner-time, several visitors would have arrived and there would not be enough to go round. 'We'll have the hen first thing,' Da had said some years ago, 'and like that the family will be sure of getting some!'

'I'll not mind any of the hen-meat just now,' Ma said to Da who was cutting it up. 'I'm not very hungry in the mornings since I don't go out to the milking.'

They all knew well enough that she just could not bring herself to eat any of her pet hens but it took Katy to say it. 'The hen will never know you ate it now, Ma,' she said suddenly, 'will it?'

'Now then Kate, that'll just do!' Da checked her with his knife and fork upright in his hand. 'Eat up your breakfast and let your Ma manage hers as she thinks best!'

After breakfast Da lit the fire in the girls' room so that they could stay there if the kitchen became too full of visitors. Aggie helped Ma with the dishes and Robert fed the hens, while John filled the coal cans and brought in armfuls of wood for the fires so that there would be little running during the day. The house began to warm up and the flowers of frost that patterned the windows were beginning to melt.

'Here's Cousin John!' Katy announced, as a bike drew up at the door. 'He's the first footer! It's a good thing it's not Nathan Thomson!'

Cousin John received a great welcome as he was a dark man, which was considered lucky in a first footer, while red-haired men, Nathan Thomson being one, were considered unlucky. And the worst of all was a red-haired woman.

Everybody wished Cousin John a Happy New Year and then, setting his long thin self on a chair by the fire, he pulled a flat half-bottle of whisky from his jacket pocket.

'A wee dram, David, for the coldest New Year I remember!' he said to Da, 'and what about you boys, Robert and John?'

'They only drink ginger wine and tea,' Katy put in quickly. 'They promised the bishop.'

'It's a good thing you're here, my Rowan Tree, to keep us all straight,' laughed Cousin John, giving her a playful skelp. 'All right boys, let it be ginger wine for a year or two yet!'

'Agnes!' Ma made signs. 'You go down the room with Katy and Jane. Keep them away from the fire.'

The fire was burning brightly and Aggie placed the three wooden stools round it and got out the picture books and the catalogue. Before sitting down she looked out of the window, which was beginning to clear round the edges.

'Maybe Robert or John will go for a walk round the fields after the dinner!' she mused, looking at the bare trees of the Far Orchard through a small clear space. 'It's a long time since I had a good walk round the fields.'

'I suppose somebody will talk about Jamie Watson's christening,' Katy grumbled as she thumbed the catalogue. 'Aggie, do you wish we had a piano?'

'Yes I do that!' Aggie replied as she turned away from the window. 'We have plenty of room for it.'

As she spoke she looked round the big bare room with the red-tiled floor. In one corner was the bed with the brass knobs on the ends and the chest of drawers close by. In another corner was a table where the books were piled, with a framed picture of Jock o'Hazeldean hanging on the wall above. On the opposite wall was a picture of the Saints ascending to Heaven surrounded by several fat little angels pointing upwards. In the wallpaper which was pink and blue roses on a yellow ground, could be seen hosts of other pictures, for when Aggie looked long enough she could pick out lines of faces with fat cheeks, long noses and round chins, all the way up the wall.

'Some folk are lucky,' Katy said. 'Cathie Gemmell has a piano and she gets music lessons.'

'Listen,' Janey hushed them. 'There's somebody else at the door.'

There were men's voices and a number of feet walking down the stone passage to the kitchen and then Da's voice bid them welcome. 'That was Wallie Johnstone anyway,' Katy whispered. 'I know how he trails his feet, and last year Wallie didn't come until New Year's night.'

'Well, it doesn't matter when he comes,' replied Aggie.

'Supposing Jamie Watson comes out at the same time and both of them wanting Auntie Lizzie,' argued Katy. 'They'll maybe kill each other like they do in the paper!'

'Oh!' wailed Janey, looking up from the doll that she was for ever dressing and undressing, 'Auntie Lizzie will have nobody then!'

'Katy, you shouldn't talk like that! If Mrs McMinn only heard you!' Aggie cried in a horrified voice.

'We're on our holidays,' Katy pointed out stubbornly. 'Anyway, sh! I heard a squeak!'

They strained their ears to listen and sure enough there came the faintest squeak-squeak of a bicycle needing oil coming towards the house.

'That's Jamie Watson's bike! I heard Ma say to Miss Blackwell in the byre that he doesn't oil his bike too much so that Auntie Lizzie can hear him coming!' cried Katy triumphantly. 'They didn't know I was listening!'

The bicycle squeaked louder and came up to the door. Then they heard Jamie Watson being wished a Happy New Year before the kitchen door closed again.

'Auntie Lizzie will be walking out later,' Aggie said. 'I expect she'll wear the hat with the velvet pansies on it.'

Now and again Ma came down the room to see to the fire and tell them who was in and who went out.

'Roderick McClurg just stayed five minutes,' she said. 'His sow had eleven wee pigs and they're doing fine! I said to tell Mrs McClurg we'd take a walk over when the days lengthened!'

'I wish we could sit in the kitchen, Ma,' Aggie said. 'We would see the folk too.'

'You're better here,' Ma smiled smoothing down the white calico apron that she put on for visitors. 'They're all men in there and it's too cold to go outside. Stay here a bit yet.'

'I can hear Wallie Johnstone laughing a lot,' Janey said as she tucked the doll up in the wooden cradle that had held them all as babies. 'Is somebody saying something funny?'

'Wallie would laugh at his shadow today!' Ma said, going back up to the kitchen. 'Mind the fire now!'

Later John came down and told them dinner was ready and they all joined the company in the kitchen. When Aggie sat in at the table she saw there were three extra, Cousin John, Jamie Watson and Wallie Johnstone. There was plenty of room for Jamie Watson had once put hinged flaps on the table to make it bigger when it was needed, and the wooden settle at the window held the girls as well as John.

Ma had made a big pot of soup with the hen boiling, and had put in plenty of rice, leeks and carrots and sprinklings of parsley on the top. This was followed by boiled potatoes with fried bacon and mealie pudding, and tea and scones to finish.

Everybody was enjoying the dinner and Da kept telling them all to eat up as there was plenty more. 'I've got the best wife in the whole country,' he added, to Aggie's surprise, for Da was quiet and mild and backward in showing his feelings, like all the folk in that part of the country. Nobody heard him for the visitors were all in a talkative mood too, but Aggie, stealing a quick look at the whisky bottle on the dresser, saw it was down a good bit. The talk round the table was mostly about the crops, the horses, the pig, the high prices, the low wages and the new motor-cars.

'Aye, David,' Cousin John said to Da, 'do you mind when I told you some time ago about the half-day for farm-workers? Well, it's going into Parliament!'

'Is that so?' Da asked.

'Aye, bar hay and harvest, of course,' answered Cousin John. 'It's not law yet, but it will likely come in after the next harvest.'

'That's something to look forward to,' Da said. 'Something more on your plate, Jamie?'

'No thanks, David,' Jamie replied, stroking his fair moustache. 'I'm doing fine. The lassies are sitting very quiet this day,' he added, looking at Aggie and her sisters.

'They know how to behave,' Ma replied, paying a warning tribute to their good manners. 'Agnes is twelve this incoming summer!'

Aggie reddened and concentrated on piling up the crumbly mealie and potatoes on the end of her fork, for Ma had always said that it was not right to eat with a knife in front of company, and the nudge from Katy's foot was not helping her any.

'Oh, the young ones will see many a thing yet,' Cousin John said, nodding his head wisely. 'There's everybody wanting a wireless now!'

'Tony Griffin has got all the bits to make one in his big shed,' Robert answered eagerly, 'and the things for your ears too! The earphones. That's for listening!'

Aggie was puzzled. She had read of wireless on ships, but what would people listen to? What would Tony Griffin hear? No wonder Mrs Gouldie was worried about the end of the world. There were queer things going on. 'I'll ask Robert later on!' she told herself.

'There are new kinds of entertainments nowadays!' Jamie Watson said knowingly. 'Just look at the pictures, for instance!'

Aggie knew all about the pictures for she had been once on a Saturday afternoon with brother John, to the little picture-house in the town. That was before he left the school. She had sat staring at the white sheet out in front until the lights went out and then all sorts of things began to happen. There were Red Indians chasing other men on horseback, a stage-coach pulled by galloping horses whizzed silently across the prairie, a ragged little man with a black moustache and a little round black hat and a walking-stick, walking with comic seriousness along a busy street, and a young woman with long fair curls had been tied to the railway-line by some bad men just as the express train was rushing round the bend towards her. As she had never been back at the pictures, Aggie often wondered what had happened to the young woman.

'We can always do with plenty of entertainment,' commented Wallie Johnstone, 'for the dear Lord only knows what this year will bring to us. Let's hope there will be no more wars like the last one, and no more sickness, and,' he added slyly 'not too many weddings!'

Cousin John roared at this, but Aggie stole a look at Jamie Watson's face. His mouth was set in a firm line, and there was no smile near it.

The dinner was over and Aggie was helping to dry the dishes when Auntie Lizzie arrived. She wore her thick navy coat and her felt hat with the purple velvet pansies in the front as Aggie had expected. She looked very splendid with the hat perched on top of her thick hair and her cheeks glowing from the cold.

'Happy New Year to you all!' she called out cheerfully, shaking hands with everybody, 'sister, and brother, and the boys and the girls, Cousin John and Jamie! And how are you, Wallie?'

'I'm just fine, Elizabeth.' Wallie stood up and Aggie could

not help liking the way his dark clean-shaven face smiled into hers. 'I can see you're fine yourself. A very Happy New Year to you!' and he held her hand tight, as his voice lingered on the last word.

'It's just like the story in the paper,' Aggie sighed to herself as she stacked up the plates.

'Let me help you off with your coat,' continued Wallie.

'Thank you, indeed!' laughed Auntie Lizzie, turning round and letting the garment slip into Wallie's hands. 'It's very kind of you.'

'That's no trouble,' answered Wallie. 'I could do this ten times a day!'

'I think it's time we had a song!' Cousin John called out quickly, when Auntie Lizzie went down the room with her things. 'Where's Katy?'

'Here!' called out Katy bouncing forward.

'Katy, what about 'The Lea Rig?''

Katy was only too willing, for all this was fun to her. Outside among strangers was another matter, but here at home she enjoyed it. Cousin John lifted her on to a chair and stood beside her, clearing his throat.

'I'm going for a walk through the fields,' Robert whispered in Aggie's ear. 'You'd better ask Ma first, if you can come. It looks bad if too many of us go out.'

'All right,' Ma whispered back, while everybody was settling themselves in a ring round the fire. 'Put on your school boots and plenty of clothes, and don't stay out too long.'

As they closed the door behind them a few minutes later, the first lines of the song followed them:

> 'It's ower yon hills the eastern star,
>   Tells buchtin' time is near, my jo,'

fading as they crossed the lane to the gate.

Outside in the fields the sun was shining and the frost glittered between the tufts of grass. The air was clear and cold and the snowy hills, sloping down towards the bay, looked like folds of pale blue velvet. The big hills beyond the town were gleaming white but the sides of Cairnsmore-of-Fleet had dark streaks where the sun had melted the snow on the rocky ledges.

'Which way are you going, Robert?' Aggie asked.

'We'll cross to the Far Orchard and go round the big loop of the river,' her brother answered. 'I can't stand being in the house the whole day. It's all right for a short while but I'm glad to get out.'

'Do you not think the stirks are making an awful noise?' Aggie asked suddenly. 'And they're not to be seen. They must be down by the river.'

'Listen!' Robert stood up and tilted his cap on the back of his head. 'There is a lot of moo-ing somewhere.'

Breaking into a trot they ran towards the edge of the field and there before them lay a wide curve of the river.

'There they are!' shouted Aggie. 'And there's some in the sands! Oh, the poor things!'

Clambering down the steep bank, they stepped among the withered canes of the reeds that grew thickly along both sides of the river. Beyond the reeds was a stretch of wet though firm sand which became softer as it sloped down to the water. It was in the soft sinking sand that two of the stirks had got stuck and the rest were running up and down on the safe patch, bellowing with fear.

'We'd better go back and tell Da, for I can do nothing with my Sunday clothes on,' Robert said. 'It's a good thing it's low tide. If the beasts had the sense to stop struggling, for it just makes them sink deeper! Hi, there! Shooop!' And he began to chase the rest of the stirks up the bank back into the field.

Aggie shuddered as she looked back at the two remaining animals, who were now almost beside themselves with panic when they saw their kind deserting them. Farther out in the middle of the river lay another sandbank in which was embedded the trunk of a tree. It looked like a black monster waiting for the tides which would release it and trap it again and again, or throw it up on the river bank among the reeds, or carry it at last on down to the bay.

'Come on, Aggie!' Robert called out. 'We can't afford to waste time.'

Aggie scurried up the slopes as though the river was at her heels. When they arrived back home, everybody was roaring with laughter at Cousin John's recitations, for he was the best of company and was much in demand at weddings and celebrations.

'Da!' Aggie yelled breathlessly, 'there's two stirks in the sands!'

'Stuck fast!' said Robert, pushing on through the kitchen.

Cousin John's words faded away and there was a moment's complete silence.

'My goodness, that's terrible!' exclaimed Da, getting to his feet as he realized what they were saying. 'In the sands, you say? I'd better go and try to get them out! Where's Robert?'

'Getting into my old clothes!' his son called out from the little bedroom at the back that he shared with John.

'I'd better do the same. Whereabouts on the sands?' Da asked Aggie on his way into the pantry.

'This side of the Far Orchard. The tide's low but the beasts are scared.'

'Robert!' Da called out. 'When you're ready, go up to the house and tell Andrew Blackwell. Then harness a horse and cart, fill it with straw and bags, and bring the big hank of new rope that's hanging up in the stable. John will go and give you a hand.'

'Oh, but we'll come and help you too!' cried Cousin John.

'Most certainly,' agreed Wallie and Jamie together.

'That's very kind of you,' Da said, coming out of the pantry in his working clothes. 'I'll be glad of your help, but get out of your good things. The wife will find you some old ones to change into. This is a cold dirty job and a wet one too!'

'A little water will not harm me,' Wallie Johnstone

announced, 'nor a lot either! For that matter,' he said in a louder voice as he turned to Auntie Lizzie, 'I'd be willing to be half-drowned if it pleasured somebody!'

Jamie Watson stood still for a minute and looked him full in the face. 'It would pleasure me,' he answered in an even voice, and turning away he strode outside.

After that Aggie felt that something in the day had changed. It was not the breaking up of the friendly cheer to get the stirks out of the sands that did it either, for that was something that the men took in their stride, like the long harvest days or waiting for the mare to foal in the night. Aggie guessed it was just something that lay between Wallie Johnstone and Jamie Watson.

For all that, they worked together in the raw cold afternoon to get the animals free, laying down the straw and the two flat wooden gates and then more straw so that Da and Andrew Blackwell could get close enough with ropes and spades.

Once Andrew Blackwell's foot caught and he nearly slipped into the water. 'That's one of the deepest pools in the river. I should know!' Wallie Johnstone told him with a grin when he was safe again. 'My grandfather used to say that in days gone by, before the bay got silted up, the coast traders used to come up the river as far as here. There was a landing-place just along there at the Far Orchard. You see the stones yet where the old house stood at the top of the bank.'

All this was news to Aggie, standing among the reeds, chattering with cold, yet not wishing to move until the stirks were out of the sands.

'I quite believe that,' Andrew Blackwell said, 'for I've heard my forefolk say much the same thing. There's no doubt there was a dwelling-house here at one time in the Orchard. Nobody plants apple trees and cherries in a field unless there's a habitation. Tell us when you're ready, David!'

'Right everybody!' Da panted for he was lying on his stomach. 'I've got this one well roped up!'

Pulling and hauling, with the stirk struggling and the sand sucking and slobbering, and then one was free. Robert and John rubbed it down with straw and sacks before the rope was taken off, and in a few minutes it had rejoined the herd who were watching the goings-on from a safe distance.

It was getting colder now for the sun, sinking behind the Barrhill in a red glare, was taking any warmth with it. An icy wind sprang up as the tide began to flow, quietly and gently, just the merest ripple, but Aggie saw the water creeping higher and higher until the old tree-trunk was nearly covered.

Then the other beast was out and Andrew Blackwell was thanking the men. 'I'm very sorry your New Year has been spoiled,' he said gravely, 'but I'm very grateful and I'll remember ye all at a more fitting time.'

'Not at all,' answered Da, flapping his hands to warm them. 'I'm pleased we got the beasts out. That's an awful death for any poor thing. It's a good job Robert and Agnes took that walk!'

'We were just in time, I'm thinking,' said Cousin John, 'Look where the tide is already!'

'Aye. It comes up steady and certain,' replied Da. 'But I think we'll away to get some tea to heat us up. Mercy, Agnes, you're frozen there! Come on to the house, quick!'

As she climbed up the slopes, Aggie turned again to the river for Wallie Johnstone's words had stayed in her mind. 'No wonder the water is so mournful looking,' she thought. 'It used to carry boats and people and now it's all choked up with the sand!'

When Da crossed the field with Cousin John and Wallie and Jamie, for the boys had gone up to the farm with Mr Blackwell to stable the horse, Aggie walked behind them so that she was sheltered from the little biting wind that was blowing.

Ma and Auntie Lizzie had the table all laid for the tea, and Aggie never saw such a welcome sight as the roaring fire and the frying-pan sizzling with eggs and potato scones.

Ma scolded her for staying out in the cold, as she had expected, then she poured her out a cup of hot tea and went to see that the men had plenty of water to wash in.

But the cheer had gone out of the house and a heavy quietness had taken its place. When Aggie heard Wallie Johnstone refuse Ma's invitation to stay for his tea, she thought the heaviness would leave the house along with him.

'No thank you, Mrs Kenny,' he said to Ma. 'My old mother will be wondering where I have been all this time, this being New Year's Day. I know she'll think the worst, so I'll get along home to pacify her! Thank you all the same. And good-night to everybody! Good-night!'

After he left Aggie heard Auntie Lizzie and Jamie Watson in conversation in the lobby. They were both talking at once in loud whispers and Ma's hand came smartly across Katy's, who was sitting with her mouth and eyes wide open trying to catch what they were saying. At this Cousin John blew his nose loudly into his red-spotted handkerchief and Aggie guessed it was to keep himself from laughing out loud.

Cousin John knew nothing of courting or love. His mother had died when he was born and Grandma Breen had brought him up, for his father, who was Ma's brother, lived in another part of the country. He was a popular 'best man' at weddings, and if any lady needed a reliable escort to see her home, Cousin John was the man, for as he said himself, he loved them all.

When the tea was over Auntie Lizzie got ready to go back home. 'Maybe, Cousin John, you'll walk into the town with me,' she said, buttoning up her coat.

There was a surprised silence.

'It has always been my habit to see you safely home, Lisbeth,' Jamie Watson said with dignity, and Aggie remembered that she had heard him use that name before, away back in the harvest time. 'And I shall take the pleasure this evening yet!'

Aggie was dismayed. Never had she heard Auntie Lizzie and Jamie Watson speak like that to each other. They were

like two strangers. What was wrong today? This was New
Year's Day—'Should Auld Acquaintance be Forgot'. Last
New Year they had all sung that together when the visitors
were setting off home. But last New Year Wallie Johnstone
had come to the house only after Auntie Lizzie had gone—
as Katy had said.

In silence she saw Jamie and Auntie Lizzie set off in the
cold starry darkness, he wheeling his squeaky bike and
Auntie Lizzie clutching her coat with both hands, instead
of putting one through Jamie's arm as was her habit.

Cousin John left sometime later and the family gathered
round the fire in thoughtful silence. There was a frown on
Ma's face as she looked into the flames and Aggie could
guess what was in her mind. 'It's just like when the pig died,'
Katy said suddenly to everybody. 'Nobody's speaking!'

They all looked at her and the boys laughed.

'I'll get out the draughts, Kate,' John said, 'and we'll have
a game, eh?'

Just then a knock came to the door and when Robert
went to answer it, Aggie heard Nathan Thomson's voice. 'I
just stepped by to wish ye all the Greetings of the day,' he
said richly. 'A Happy New Year to ye all!'

'The same to you, Nathan!' Da replied in his friendliest
tones. 'Draw a chair up to the fire, for it's a very cold night.'

Aggie sighed with relief for he, she thought, would
console anybody.

Chapter Eight

ON THE day after New Year, which was still a holiday, Da and the boys took the train to Grandmother and Grandfather Kenny's to wish them the Best of Everything in the New Year. Aggie would have liked to have gone too, for the train journey was exciting although it only lasted an hour and then there was the long walk up the wide street of Da's own town.

'No, no, Agnes!' Ma said. 'Da and your brothers are plenty for your grandmother to deal with. She and your grandfather are well over seventy and they're not so fit to deal with a lot of visitors. Besides, I said to your Auntie Lizzie yesterday that I might walk in to the Old Village with you girls for a change!'

That satisfied Aggie, for at least she was going somewhere. She knew too that Ma had her own thoughts about Grandfather Kenny, for she used to say that he did not believe in anything.

Aggie could have told Ma otherwise but she had no idea how to tell it. It had been in the summertime after the field work was over, that Aggie and her sisters had stayed with the Kenny grandparents for a few days. It was the first time they had been away from home by themselves and Ma had walked in to the station with them that warm summer day, to put them on the train.

'Mind and behave yourselves now, and don't touch the carriage door or put your head out of the window!' she warned them.

'When do we know we're there, Ma?' asked Aggie for the tenth time.

'The name of the place is written on a big board at every station,' Ma explained patiently.

'Supposing the train doesn't stop at the station, Ma,' said Katy, and Aggie had visions of the train whooping along the line at great speed with no intention of ever stopping.

'There's no fear of that at all,' Ma replied, mopping the sweat off her face with her handkerchief. 'Your station is at the end of the line so the train cannot go any further. Now Agnes, look after your sisters, help your grandmother all you can, and don't lose the tickets!'

'Yes, Ma.'

'As for the church on Sunday,' Ma continued, 'I don't know what your grandfather will do, I'm sure.'

On the Sunday Grandfather Kenny did what he had done on the other days they were there, took the three girls out of the town into the fields.

'I don't know how to say prayers in that big building in front of all the folk,' he said to Aggie, as he squirted tobacco juice neatly out of the side of his mouth, 'and I can't get down on my knees for my rheumatics, but just look at this!' Slowly he stooped and picked up a daisy. 'There is the bonniest thing,' he said, 'and you'll hear them say, "it's just a daisy". But when I meet a man that can create something like this, I'll listen to all he has to tell me!'

He looked up at the wide blue sky as Aggie and Katy and Janey watched him with awe, 'And you're likelier to find the Creator here than in the church!' he added, walking slowly away with his hands behind him.

Grandfather Kenny took slow ponderous steps but they were not aimless. He plodded through fields and woods and along cattle tracks, talking of the wild life as Aggie had never heard before.

'It's only when you're old like me,' he twinkled at her, 'that you wish you had taken the time to look at all this long before now!'

One day they reached the shore. It was the first time Aggie had been close to the sea and it was the most wondrous sight she had seen in all her life. The great waves came rolling and hissing up the beach and when the water fell back the little pink shells and round pebbles rocked in the wash until the next wave curled back over them again. Far over the tumbling waters was a faint blue line of land.

'That's Ireland!' Grandfather Kenny told them with a sly smile. 'Ah, but there used to be a deal of smuggling going on between the two!'

All these things passed through Aggie's mind as she watched Da and the boys go up the road in the frosty cold and she guessed it would be too hard to explain to Ma or anybody else about God in the fields or on the seashore.

'Agnes, come on in now!' Ma called out. 'There's a lot of cleaning up to be done before we reach Grandma's!'

Aggie raced back inside, for it was not often that Ma had the chance to go visiting; either she had to be back for the milking or else the weather was bad.

But today there was no milking to bother about and the sun was shining through the frost on the roads, which were as dry and firm as the kitchen floor.

'Mind, I've got to be back before darkening, as I'll have to shut up the hens myself. Da will not be home until about eight tonight,' Ma warned Aggie, 'so the sooner we're away the better!'

Aggie set to the making of the beds along with Katy, then she plaited Janey's hair and fastened her button boots. All the while her mind was full of thoughts of Auntie Lizzie, whose heart was now most certainly broken.

'I wonder if she wept all the night,' Aggie thought to herself as she buttoned her own boots in the cold room. 'I wonder if her pillow was drowned in tears like the one in "Afraid to Love him".' She and Katy had gone into this very thoroughly last night before they fell asleep, and Ma and Da had been too busy entertaining Nathan Thomson to hear them.

Picking up her woollen tammy she pulled it fiercely down on to her head. 'Wallie Johnstone would have been better to have kept his Happy New Year to himself,' she muttered as she went along the passage for her coat. 'Katy's clever. She said he'd bring trouble and he did!'

'My, Agnes,' Ma greeted her with an anxious frown. 'I declare your coat will soon be too small for you. Pull the sleeves down a bit!'

'They'll not go any further, Ma,' Aggie replied, tugging at them. 'I expect I'm growing again. I wish I could stop!'

'You shouldn't wish anything like that, Agnes!' Ma said sharply. 'You're not that tall, and the winter is half over anyway. Your coat will see you through the rest of it.'

'Don't pull the sleeves too hard and tear them, Aggie!' Katy told her, 'for I have to wear that coat next year!'

'Oh, Ma, will I have to put it on when Katy grows out of it?' Janey inquired.

'My goodness, I hope not, but you never can tell,' Ma said in a harassed kind of voice, as she fastened her navy felt hat on her head with a large hatpin. 'Are you all ready?'

'Yes, Ma!' they chorussed brightly, flocking outside.

Ma looked round the kitchen to see that the cats were out and that the fire was safely banked up with smush so that it would smoulder slowly until their return. Satisfied that everything was as it should be she went outside, locked the door behind her and put the key below the stone at the edge of the flower border.

'It's a bonnie day!' she remarked, looking round. 'I don't think the frost is just as hard,' although their breaths were making little clouds around them.

The rime glistened and sparkled in the cold gleam of the sun, on every blade of grass and twig and withered leaf and on the little rough stones of the lane. In the big sauch trees a colony of rooks gathered and caw-cawed to each other watched by several thoughtful seagulls perched coldly on the frosty roof of one of the farmhouse steadings.

'The Kennys are out in full force this day!' Miss Blackwell called out to them. 'I saw David and the boys passing by a wee while ago.'

'They're away to visit the father's folk,' Ma answered, 'and the girls and me are going into Grandma's. It's not often a body gets the chance!'

'That's true!' Miss Blackwell agreed. 'If it wasn't for my bad leg, I'd be away oftener too!'

'Now what would make you want to roam the countryside?' her brother shouted from where he was washing the milkcans. 'It's warmer in the house.'

'Everybody needs a change and you get plenty, with your markets and meetings and curling!' retorted his sister. 'Andrew Blackwell thinks a woman should never be out of the house,' she said to Ma. 'One of these days he's in for a big surprise!'

'There's nothing I like better than a surprise,' he laughed, 'and the bigger, the better!'

Miss Blackwell and Ma smiled to each other and the Kennys moved off.

'What kind of a surprise will it be, Ma?' Janey wanted to know.

'Oh, that was just talk,' Ma answered. 'Katy, stop that sliding for you know what your father will say when he looks at the soles of your boots!'

If Aggie had expected to see Auntie Lizzie drooping and pining, she was very mistaken for Grandma's kitchen was full of visitors and she was seated among them enjoying the company. As well as Cousin John, there were three uncles, brothers of Ma, all spending the New Year holiday with Grandma and Granda. The noise was uproarious for everybody was talking and laughing and Granda Breen was banging away with his stick and doing his best to shout them all down.

Room was made for Ma and the girls and ginger wine and cake were brought out, for Granda did not believe that women should have strong drink.

'I think Auntie Lizzie must have made it up with Jamie!' Katy managed to whisper to Aggie as they emptied their glasses.

Aggie nodded. Auntie Lizzie would not be joking with her brothers like that if her heart were breaking. Then the table was set for the tea and Aggie noticed that Grandma and Ma had disappeared and she could hear the murmur of their voices down the room. Nobody could have heard their conversation for Granda Breen was shouting about the short skirts that women were now wearing. 'Getting their hair cut and having votes and all, and jumping out and in aeryeo-planes!' he roared, 'and showing their knees forbye! What is the world coming to? They'll be wearing trousers next!'

At this Cousin John and the uncles shouted with laughter and Katy and Janey kicked their heels against the chair legs in delighted merriment.

'Father,' Auntie Lizzie said calmly as she reached up to the mantelpiece for the tea-caddy, 'men have been showing their knees since the world started, and it has not been of much benefit! Maybe a change will help!'

'Don't contradict your father, woman!' he howled at her. 'What I say is right!'

Auntie Lizzie patted his cheek for she never took offence at his roaring, knowing that in his eyes she was still a little girl.

It was a cheerful afternoon with Cousin John at his merriest and the Uncles relating about their families and Ma enjoying it all. Later on, going out the road in the frosty cold with Ma and her sisters, Aggie thought how good it was that everything was as usual between Auntie Lizzie and

Jamie and how silly she and Katy had been with all their nonsense about aching hearts. Just to make sure she asked Ma.

'Oh no,' Ma answered sadly, 'everything is not all right. Auntie Lizzie said to your Grandma that she wouldn't be seeing Jamie Watson for a long time.'

'But, Ma,' Aggie persisted, 'she—she was carrying on and joking like all the rest.'

'Aye, so she was,' agreed Ma, 'but your Auntie Lizzie is not one to show what she's feeling. Give me your hand, Janey. Agnes will take your other one.'

'Oh well,' said Katy with a kind of gulp, 'Granda will be pleased anyway.'

'Granda doesn't know,' Ma replied. 'He'll not be that pleased either for he likes Jamie Watson well enough as a man. He just will not consent to a marriage till Jamie's been christened.'

'It's all Wallie Johnstone's fault!' announced Katy from the other side of Ma.

Aggie shivered. It was freezing again and she had a feeling that the frost was falling on her. The warmth and pleasure of the day was being spoiled.

'I think the wind's changing,' Ma remarked. 'I hope it thaws before the school starts on Tuesday.'

'Oh don't say anything about the school, Ma!' begged Katy. 'There's a whole week-end yet!'

'The happiest days of your life are your school-days!' Ma consoled her brightly. 'I think we'll just manage home before darkening.'

'Anyway,' thought Aggie to herself, 'it has been nice to be out visiting with Ma. But I think she doesn't want to say too much to us about Auntie Lizzie!'

There was plenty to do in the next few days before the school started. The christmas cards were put away, the New Year calendars hung up and Ma gave Aggie their long black school stockings to darn. The feet were already thick with darns, but that all helped to keep the cold out.

Aggie went back over the homework which Mrs McMinn had given her to do, and Ma made Katy and Janey read out loud from their reading-books, while she was baking the scones.

Katy was agreeable to this as she said it might save her getting a slap with the cane the first day at least.

The cold eased off as the wind softened, and the sky became grey and overcast. 'It looks like snow,' Da said, 'I'd better have a look at your boots before the school starts.'

Katy especially dreaded Da's boot inspection; She always put off telling him when one of the iron shods came off as she was supposed to, for she liked the soft footfall of the leather without the heavy clamp of the tackets.

Da's prophecy came true and on the day the school started, they set off in a flurry of snow.

'I wouldn't send you but I don't think it will snow much,' Ma said to them. 'It's more like showers than a fall.'

Ma made a lonely figure as she waved to them, when they turned round for the last time before the road dipped into the Hollow, with the snowflakes flying round her in a whirling veil.

They hesitated for a moment. 'Ta-ta, Ma!' they shouted and then she was no longer in sight.

'I'll never get my hair cut, ever!' Aggie mumbled to herself, for that was the only thing at the moment which she reckoned would please Ma the most, and she was glad of the snow's sharp sting, for it helped to keep the tears from rising. Then the sky cleared and it stopped snowing.

'Aggie, we can slide on this!' Katy cried as she flew along a smooth cart track, then turning round, she asked suddenly, 'Oh, Aggie, have you forgotten about the Qualifying, now?'

'No, and I've tried to!' Aggie groaned, and the fun of the snow disappeared. 'January, February, March, and then April! It's not very long now! And supposing I don't pass!'

'The Doctor said you would pass,' Janey called out, 'and he knows everything!'

'They've all got on the same things at the High School,'

Katy said, 'even the hats. A hat like that will be a change from a woollen tammy, eh, Aggie!'

'I like Auntie Lizzie's hats best,' Janey decided.

'Oh, Aggie, what will we say when folk ask us about Auntie Lizzie's marriage now?' Katy then wanted to know.

'Say we don't know,' answered Aggie.

'That's a lie!' Janey's comment from the back was sharp. 'We know that Auntie Lizzie is not speaking to Jamie, and nobody can get married if they're not speaking to each other!'

'And John says if she married Wallie Johnstone, the policeman will never be left the door!' retorted Katy.

'The policeman!' echoed Janey. 'What for?'

'Mm!' Katy's voice dropped to a whisper although there was not a soul in sight. 'Wallie's poaching is against the law!'

'The best thing is to say we don't know anything about it,' Aggie said firmly, 'for we don't.'

'Well, I hope Jamie Watson's heart's broken anyway!' Katy said fiercely, 'and his hair is not nearly as curly as Wallie's.'

'Oh, Katy, I don't like that!' Janey wailed, for the human emotions worried her. 'Aggie, tell her to stop!'

As Aggie took her little sister's hand, they all lapsed into silence for the ending of Auntie Lizzie's romance, which they had been used to all their days, made them uneasy.

The light covering of snow had changed the Little Valley and the surrounding hills from a picture of wintry bleakness to the delicate lines of a Christmas card. The long black thorn spikes of the hedges were edged with white and the dark green whins leaning against the snow-topped dike were daubed with snow-flakes.

'If I scraped below the snow at the foot of that thorn bush, I'd find the snowdrops up,' Aggie said just before they joined the big road.

'Yes, they were there last year. And in the Little Wood too!' Katy agreed eagerly. 'Oh, isn't everything quiet and soft!'

'Mm,' said her sister, 'and here's another shower!'

Under the covering of snow, the town too looked different. The church with the tall spire, grey and solemn all the year round, now bore a look of fragile purity, and the houses, huddling shoulder to shoulder, might have come out of a fairy tale. The layer of white ice, that had gathered along the edges of the river, made the water flowing in the channel between look dark and menacing.

In the streets the milk-carts and wagons made muffled sounds, but the fishmonger's motor-van came jangling along with chains on the wheels.

'John says they put those things on to keep them from slipping,' Katy explained, for she followed her brother's mechanical discoveries closely.

Outside the school gates they could hear Mrs McMinn's voice and Aggie reckoned that today's fall of snow had not served to soften it any.

'Good morning Agnes, Katherine and Mary Jane!' the teacher greeted them and Aggie knew that a period of training in good manners lay ahead.

'Good morning, ma'am,' they mumbled in return.

'Speak up now, girls,' Mrs McMinn urged them. 'That's not the way to answer. Now everybody in the school, attention please! All together, say "Good morning, ma'am"!'

'Good morning, ma'am!' they roared.

'That's better. Never forget that good manners are one of the most important things in life!' she said as she reached for the register.

After prayers she announced that the Qualifying Class was going to receive her special attention, as was the religious instruction of the whole school. More care must be taken with good manners and each pupil had to learn a new piece of recitation for the visit of the Inspector, which she was sure would take place any day.

As usual it took Aggie the whole forenoon to get into stride again. Her thoughts kept wandering from Ma, now at home by herself, to Auntie Lizzie, then to the sums in front of her and back again to Helen McKay's new blue jumper. And all the time she was aware of Mrs McMinn's canings and threats, of smarting knuckles and stinging hands.

At the morning break it snowed again and most of the children huddled in the porch. Aggie listened with great interest to Cathie Gemmell and Helen McKay reciting their Christmas presents, which included beads and scent and boxes of chocolates.

'We all had presents in our house too,' she told them when they asked about Christmas Day at home, and hoped they would ask no more questions for this was only half true.

'So had we,' Eddie Campbell joined in, for he had been listening open-mouthed. 'And if you come outside, Cathie Gemmell, I'll give you another one! I'll rub your face with snow!'

Aggie hid a smile for she felt that Eddie took a delight in shocking the others. He was as ragged and cheerful as ever and his pockets were stuffed as before with lumps of his grandmother's treacle toffee wrapped up in newspaper.

At dinner-time the sky was grey, but the snow had left off falling.

Aggie thought that both her grandparents were a little quiet, for Granda sat for quite a long minute after they were in, with his chin leaning on his hands, folded over the crook of his stick.

Suddenly he turned to them and demanded, 'How's your father getting on with the new pig-house?'

'It's nearly finished!' Aggie answered.

'And Roddie McClurg's pig will be ready in February,' Katy put in.

'Mm!' Granda growled. 'Jamie Watson will have plenty of spare time on his hands now, I'm thinking. Not that I care!' he ended with a roar.

'We can all hear you without shouting,' Grandma chided him. 'Eat up, Agnes. You're growing fast. How is Mrs McMinn today?'

'Just the same,' Aggie replied gloomily.

'She's a fine teacher,' Grandma answered. 'And she means

very well. Don't work against her, Agnes. Work along with her. Bend to the storm, wee lass, like the reeds!'

Aggie blinked away the sudden tears that were always so ready to spring up, and the tension of the morning left her. She gulped and nodded, for Grandma's little round face was so wise and kind and she never raised her voice.

'And who's going to convoy your Auntie Lizzie back home these nights?' Granda wanted to know, and Aggie sensed that he knew all about the broken romance.

'She'll come in with John on his way to the night-school!' Grandma replied. 'I'm sure she told you herself.'

'So long as it's not that poacher! I can't abide heathens but poachers are a deal worse!' he shouted, then heaving a deep sigh, he sank his chin once more on his hands.

'He would rather have Jamie Watson any day,' Grandma said at the door as she handed Aggie the little bag of sweets. 'But things will work themselves out.'

'The course of true love never does run smooth!' said Katy unexpectedly.

'Aggie saw that in the paper, Grandma!' Janey told her proudly. 'She read it out to us! Sometimes she reads us the story if she can find nothing else!'

Grandma laughed until the water came squeezing out from between her bright little eyes.

'You shouldn't be reading that at your age!' she managed to say at last, as she wiped her eyes with her apron. 'I'll see if I can't borrow some books from somebody. My, that sky is full of snow! Mind and ask the teacher to let you away, if it comes on thick!'

A cold little wind was now blowing and some pearls of snow were flying before it. The flakes had changed from the soft ones of the morning to little stinging ones that came from the direction of the hills in the north.

Up the school hill, the girls were pelted with snowballs which they returned, and when the bell rang for classes, they were all as warm as pies and looking like snowmen. The wind had increased and flakes were now coming down faster

and thicker. Aggie could hear them smacking against the
school windows, which became so thickly crusted with snow,
and made the light so dim, that Mrs McMinn lit the gas
jets that hung down from the ceiling.

Aggie tried hard to forget the falling snow and concentrate
on her lessons. All her interest had returned since Grandma
had counselled her and she felt that Mrs McMinn had
sensed this too.

'Agnes!' the teacher said after she had gone over her sums,
'your arithmetic shows a marked improvement, I'm pleased
to say. Try and keep it up by doing as much as you can at
home. Now, as it's snowing quite heavily, I think you and
your sisters ought to leave in case it gets any worse. Wrap
Mary Jane up well and remember to wear your oilskins.'

Aggie packed up her books with a very thoughtful feeling,
for, although the South-West had not great snowfalls every
winter, yet there had been times when storms had come up,
blocking the roads and burying the lanes in deep drifts for
days.

'The first day of the school and we're out already!' Katy
whispered gleefully, as they put on their coats in the porch.

'It's just as well,' answered Aggie. 'It's coming down
heavy. Oh, Janey, your gloves are soaking!'

'That was the snowballs,' Janey replied.

'You should always play snowballs with your bare hands,
Janey! Oh well,' sighed Aggie, 'wear one of mine and one of
Katy's. We'll keep one hand in a pocket.'

'The pocket of an oilskin coat isn't very warm,' complained
Katy.

Bundled up in their oilskins with the yellow sou'westers
pulled well down over their faces, and tied below the chin,
they set off down the hill. The few people in the street were
scurrying along close to the houses, hastening to finish their
business before the snow got too deep.

'Hurry on home now, lassies!' the stout grocer who had
his shop at the foot of the hill, warned them. 'Don't waste
any time on the road!'

'Yes, Mr Paterson,' Aggie answered, for that was where she got any messages that Ma needed during the week.

'It would be nice to live in the town when the weather was bad, Aggie,' Katy said to her, 'but then we'd never get out early!'

'Aggie, it makes my face sore,' Janey complained as they crossed the bridge with the snow driving into them.

'Hold your head down, Janey,' Aggie said. 'It will be better when we get in the lee of the Big Wall. Keep hold of Katy and me!'

Once out on the Big Road the wind was on their backs. It came in strong gusts, sending the snow flying in pebbly clouds and piling it up already against the dike-sides. There was some shelter from the stinging flakes on the sidewalk, but when Aggie had to raise her head to see if the lane was anywhere near, the wind threshed the snow across her face with a cold fury.

At the Chestnut Wood they stopped for a moment, for Aggie reckoned that Janey's legs would be getting tired, since she had to keep on lifting them where the snow was deep. All around them whirled the snow like a never-ending swarm of bees, and it made Aggie dizzy if she looked up at it too long.

'Aggie,' Janey asked, 'if it stops snowing do we have to turn round and go back to the school?'

'Goodness, no! It's nearly half-past three already anyway,' answered Aggie, 'and we'd better move on again too!'

'Will we change sides, Aggie, so that my other hand gets the glove?' asked Katy. Aggie agreed, for the hand she had to keep in her oilskin pocket was nearly frozen too.

Leaving the shelter of the Chestnut Wood they bent their heads and set off once more.

They were almost at the lane when they heard the chains of a motor-car clanking behind them. It was the Doctor, and, honking his horn twice to let them know he knew them, he zig-zagged on his way along the Big Road between the drifts, soon disappearing in the snowy distance.

'There's more than us out today!' Katy shouted to Aggie above the wind as they entered the lane. There in the narrow lane the drifts were deeper, with the snow piled half-way up the hedge in one place and smoothly covering the lane in another.

They were near the Little Wood when a snowy figure came out of the swarming flakes.

'It's Ma!' cried Katy. 'Oh, Ma!'

'My, that's a cold blast! I could hardly raise my head to see coming along there!' she panted. 'I thought I would meet you in case the teacher didn't think to let you away, and you could easily miss the turning of the lane in this storm!'

'It's not so bad with your back to it, Ma!' Aggie answered, 'but the teacher saw it was getting worse so she let us go.'

'The doctor's out in it too,' Janey said. 'Ma, my legs are tired!'

'Well, we haven't far to go before we get back home now,' Ma answered. 'We'll hurry on as there's not much daylight left.'

As they set off along the lane, the branches of the trees in the Little Wood waved and creaked as the snow hissed against them, driven by the freezing wind.

At home Ma brought in plenty of coals and wood, while Aggie and Katy carried buckets of water between them into the house in case the snowstorm lasted. There was no use waiting for Da and the boys to do it for they would not be home till after dark.

All that evening the wind whistled round the house and the snow slushed against the walls. Da looked out at bed-time and said that a great drift of snow lay across the lane, burying the gate and the pump and a lot of the hedge. When Aggie awoke in the morning it was to a white and silent world.

Many times in her life she had heard Ma and Da tell their stories of the Big Snow of their childhood. Houses had been isolated and animals buried for weeks; people had lost their lives.

Standing in the lane where Da and the boys had cleared a path, she remembered this now for all she could see were the tops of hedges and round hills of snow where, before, there had been flat fields.

'You're not going to the school today, Agnes,' Ma said, 'you wouldn't be able to get far up the lane. Da had to dig his way up to the farm. It's a good thing, I'm still not milking!'

This suited them all, especially Katy, who spent most of the time shovelling the snow away from the door and making it into a snowman, finishing off her creation with an old cap of Robert's, to Janey's great admiration. The sun came out and the snow on the roof began to melt, which in the afternoon froze again, making a long row of pointed icicles hanging from the eaves like a crystal frieze.

It was several days before school was mentioned for Aggie developed a cold and Ma did not like to send Katy and Janey without her. Da got out the whisky bottle and made a toddy for everybody so that Aggie's cold would not spread round the family. As she sipped the sweet and fiery drink before she lay down to sleep, Aggie remembered Mrs Gouldie and she hoped that she would not be thumping with her fist and shouting as she had done. She had no time for much wondering for she slept immediately.

The hard weather came back again and everybody said it was a very severe winter and it had been a long time since the Little Valley had known such a one.

The sun shone by day and a half-moon appeared at night and the Little Valley gleamed and glittered with snow and ice, both in sunlight and moonlight. Ma went back to the milking and the girls returned to the school. Great mounds of snow were piled up at the sides of the lane but on the Big Road, the traffic had worn the highway smooth and it was the easiest thing in the world to slide along and far less trouble than walking.

Once again Auntie Lizzie started to come out on her usual visiting days, but it was queer to see her setting off home with

John on his way to the night-school, and never one word did she say about Jamie Watson.

Aggie used to watch Jamie when he came out to finish the pig-house. Never a very talkative man, yet sociable enough in his quiet way, he now just sat staring into the fire after the work was over, with the family silent around him. Ma gave up trying to make conversation for Jamie made no attempt to continue it, except when Da offered to pay him for what he had done.

'No, no, David!' he said, getting up to go. 'I said I would do it for you, and right pleased I am to be able to!'

'That's very kind of you, indeed, Jamie!' Da replied. 'I'm very grateful to you, and don't forget, you're always welcome here, so just come along when you take the notion.'

'Thank you, David,' Jamie said. 'I'll remember that.'

Jumping on his bike, which was now silent and well-oiled, he disappeared up the road.

For once, Cousin John, who was there that night, had nothing to laugh at. He looked at them all, his grey eyes very serious.

'I can hardly believe it,' he said, shaking his head, 'after all these years!'

In the meantime the frost got keener, and Aggie shivered in the church on Sundays, for that was the coldest place of all. Feeling her feet getting numb inside her boots, she tried to keep her thoughts on the service and wondered what she ought to pray for now. A thaw?

'There will be no change till this moon's out,' Da had said, 'she's a frosty one and no mistake!'

Often she wondered what Auntie Lizzie prayed for now. At one time she had a fair idea, but now things were completely out of hand. The last time Auntie Lizzie was out at the house, there had been a knock at the door and there stood Wallie Johnstone, all dressed up in his Sunday clothes, asking for the pleasure of seeing Elizabeth home. She had granted him the pleasure.

Aggie's teeth chattered. Controlling them with some effort, she managed to ask the Almighty to remember Jamie Watson, herself and the Qualifying, and all the family. She left out Wallie Johnstone on purpose.

At the church door various members of the congregation invited Da, Robert, John and herself—for Ma was at home with Katy and Janey—into their homes for tea to warm them up. Da refused with many thanks, much to the relief of Robert who was very shy in company, but it made Aggie feel a little warmer to know they had been asked. So they set off home in the cold sunlight and Aggie could not manage the shortest slide for Da kept such a strict eye on all their boots.

The hard grip of frost affected most folk in the Little Valley. The old people had to stay at home, the middle-aged ones complained of extra work for pumps were frozen, hands chapped and sore, roads were icy, washing froze on the line, horses had to wear frosters, and Da was behind with the ploughing.

Even Cousin John had something to say for all the ploughing matches were cancelled because of the hard ground, and he was a medal man and keen on the championship.

Only the young ones enjoyed it; the town children skated on the frozen river at the shallow part near the bridge, while Aggie and her sisters had a fine slide on a marshy pool that lay in a hollow in the field behind the house. It was not very big but there was a long straight runway between the frozen clumps of rushes, and Katy could slide along it and do a double turn at the end without falling. At times like these Aggie thought there was nothing better than the frost, but it was different when her feet started to get cold in the school and in church, and the chilblains on her heels were sore in the morning and itchy at night.

The moon waxed and waned and the hard snow glittered like glass. February was close at hand. 'There's no frost tonight!' Aggie, lying in bed, heard John announce as he

arrived in from the night-school and then Ma said something about it freezing in the morning very likely, before the
kitchen door was shut and she heard no more.

Next day Aggie was up early as usual, listening to Da's
warning about the kettle, the fire and the lamp. 'It's not
nearly so cold today,' he said as he left, 'it's just as well.
This frost keeps everybody behind with the work!'

Aggie washed her face and hands, and after combing and
plaiting her hair, she stood at the door to listen for Ma.
The daylight was still pale and the snow in the fields looked
grey. A light wind was blowing up from the bay like a soft
breath and now and then Aggie heard the snow fall from
the hedges in sudden little showers.

Ma's clogs crunched deeply as she came down the lane,
instead of ringing out sharply as they had done in the frost.

'Ah,' breathed Aggie, letting the damp wind blow on her
upturned face, 'the thaw has come at last!'

Chapter Nine

THE roads were slushy with melting snow and the February rain had already washed the hills and fields green again, except for a few white patches where the deep drifts had been. Aggie was used to the rain beating down on the way to school, for the skies of the south-west mostly contained more rain than either snow or sunshine. When the snowdrops appeared under the hedges and the green spears of the daffodils showed along the garden fence where Ma had planted the bulbs many years ago, it was difficult to believe that, not so long ago, the ground had been hard and ice-packed with frost.

In the ley field beyond the Far Orchard Da and Robert were both ploughing, and each trod the furrow, followed by a cloud of shrieking seagulls. The first sounds of spring began to be heard, the cry of the peewit, the early warbles of a little songbird in the hedge, and the noisy meetings held by the crows in the big sauch trees.

'The salmon are coming up the river,' Da remarked one night. 'I saw one leap today, a great big fellow he was, too!'

'He'd better hurry on,' Robert said, 'for Wallie Johnstone will be on his tracks!'

Aggie shivered. There was a time when she had thought

of Wallie as an heroic figure who could outwit the game-keeper any time. Now that he was coming closer into the family, her ideas were beginning to change, and her new vision was more sinister. There, in her mind's eye, was Wallie slinking along the ditch-sides and hedges in the dark, setting his traps, sliding the ferrets into the rabbit holes, catching the salmon with merciless cunning, and returning home before daylight with his load of death.

'There's blood on his hands!' Katy decided, when she heard Aggie's views on their way home from school.

'But we eat rabbits too!' Janey pointed out. 'Maybe Wallie Johnstone doesn't like anything else.'

'Wallie sells the rabbits for money!' Katy cried with impatience. 'He doesn't eat any of them! John told me. Oh, there's Jamie Watson back at the pighouse!'

'He said he'd come back and see how it stood up to the rain,' Aggie said, 'and on Saturday Da is going up to Roddie McClurg's for the new pig!'

Saturday was mild and fine, with the fields sobbing and sucking with the rain that had fallen, and the birds twittering and chirping gaily.

'If you're ready, you three lassies, about the middle of the afternoon,' Da said, 'you can come with me to fetch the pig. The boys will groom the horses for me.'

'Now mind your manners to Mrs McClurg,' Ma warned them as she helped Janey into her coat later on, 'and if she offers you tea say "no thank you." She's not a young woman and she has had her share of trouble.'

'Ma, maybe she'll have tea in the pot, anyway. What do we say then?'

'Oh, that's different. Then it would not do to refuse!'

'It would be better to say "yes please" the first time, Ma!' Katy put in as she pulled her woollen tammy down over her hair. 'It would save all that time!'

'You're an awful Kate!' Ma said, with a laugh as she set the tammy straight. 'Here's your father. Run on now and mind all I told you!'

Roddie McClurg lived in a little cottage at the top of the Hill Village, and to take the long road round meant a walk of two miles anyway. So Da and the girls took the short cut across the fields that went behind the house.

Da was in no hurry. He sauntered along with a sack under his arm and his three girls at his heels, and now and again he stopped to look up at the sky, dappled with the small white clouds of early spring.

When they reached the wooden plank that spanned the Gow Burn, he stepped on it heavily to test its safeness, and then led the way across.

The burn water was brown and rippled over gravel beds. In summer the forget-me-nots and marsh-marigolds bloomed along its banks and small fish swam in its waters. Sometimes on a warm Sunday afternoon Ma made up 'pieces' and took the three girls to the burn to paddle or fish, while she herself rested on the grassy bank. Aggie reckoned that Ma liked to get out of the house sometimes, with its never-ending work, and see the wide sky above her as she herself did.

After the Gow Burn, they crossed another field and there was the Big Road with the bottom half of the Hill Village strewn along the roadside at the foot of the hill. The other half was perched in a hollow at the top of the hill with a climb up a steep brae to reach it.

The last time Aggie had been in the Hill Village was in the summertime when the sun was hot and the air was heavy with the smell of whins and bracken, and the sound of bees. Now the bracken was withered and brown and only the green moss and bare heather roots showed among the rock, but there were buds on the whins.

At the top of the hill, they stopped to get back their breath and to look at the view over the valley. There was their own house standing white and alone, and then Miss Blackwell's farm, and the little round turrets of the Castle, sticking up above the trees, and the river, twisting and curving all the way down to the bay.

For a time Aggie stared down into the Little Valley with

its varied pattern of brown and green fields, and picked out
the landmarks she knew.

There was Nathan Thomson's little stone cottage where
he and his wife lived with their many children, and his old
mother, whom everybody said had the worst tongue in the
place. An avenue of trees leading to the Castle, showed
where the White Lady walked on moonlight nights, and
there at the cross-roads was the big flat stone on which the
preacher stood, when delivering his sermons on the clear
Sunday nights of the summer. Farther along the road was
the Hangman's Tree, with its big thick arm, jutting out from
the trunk and on which no moss would grow. The ghostly
moans and whispers that came from the tree on a dark night,
it was said, were terrible to hear.

The longer Aggie looked, the more she saw; the mill-dam
at the Gow Farm, with its fleet of ducks, Big Charlie trotting
through the field in the distance, a line of washing, the grey
waters of the bay, and at the foot of the hill, the broad
ribbon of the Big Road, winding its way to the grey town in
the grey distance.

This being Saturday most of the traffic was going towards
the town, but Aggie recognized the Doctor's motor-car
coming the other way.

'There's the Doctor!' Janey cried out. 'Oh, somebody
must be sick!'

'Maybe he's going to visit Lennie Hannah and her new
baby,' Katy said. 'Da, do you know what Ma told Auntie
Lizzie last week when I was in the pantry?'

'No,' Da answered idly. 'What did she say?'

'That Harry Dickson should be made to pay for that. Da,
does that mean . . .?'

'We'd better get on to Mrs McClurg's!' Da interrupted
suddenly. 'I think we've seen plenty. I doubt you took your
Ma up wrong!'

'That's what she said!' Katy insisted, as they turned back
on to the rough hill road. 'Oh, Aggie, isn't Cairnsmore close?'

The long blue hump of Cairnsmore with the snow still on

the top, lay just in front, although there was a wide glen between. Aggie stared at the rocky edges and once again wondered what lay on the other side.

'London is over there, where the train goes every night,' Katy said, reading her thoughts. 'And India and the Great War,' and she too stared for a moment with the dream in her eyes.

Mrs McClurg's house was one of a straggling row of white-washed cottages with a thatched roof. Behind the house was a long garden with a row of bee-boxes down one side and a pig-house at the far end. The road through the village, over which a stream of fresh water gurgled, wound down the back of the hill, past the country schoolhouse, into the glen, where it divided into tracks and trails, leading to the farms and cottages hidden in its remoteness.

At one time there had been lead mining carried on in the hills and the district round about was burrowed with shafts. Aggie remembered Roddie McClurg once say that he had heard the rattle of the miners' spades, working underneath his house. After that she had a terrible vision of the top half of the Hill Village disappearing into a yawning hole. However it never happened, and when the mines were closed down, the cottages still stood.

Mrs McClurg was small and very dark, and as she welcomed them in, Aggie saw the firelight winking on the brass fender and the kettle on the hob. The room was as cosy as a wren's nest.

'Roderick is expecting you,' she said to Da. 'He's down at the pig-house. I'll get a cup of tea ready if you go out to him yourself. Sit down, Agnes. My, you're fairly growing! Katy, here's a chair for you, and Janey can sit on the stool next to you.'

'Don't take the trouble to make tea for us, thank you, Mrs McClurg,' Aggie managed to say, remembering Ma's instructions and forcing herself to speak through the terrible wall of shyness that was always there.

'Goodness, that's no trouble! I'm fair pleased to see you!'

135

replied the other briskly. 'All young folk can eat and drink at any time!' and she drew a cloth out of a drawer and enveloped the table in it.

'That's true!' replied Katy agreeably. 'I'm always hungry.'

'Me, too!' Janey said in a tone that was equally friendly.

Aggie reddened and made up her mind to check Katy's and Janey's manners, when she got the chance of them by themselves. Mrs McClurg would think they had come expecting their tea and that they had nothing to eat at home.

In the meantime cups and saucers were laid on the table and a jar of honey, and a big plate of scones, butter and cheese, placed in the middle, with Mrs McClurg asking after Ma and the boys and the school all the time. Then she took a large gingerbread with a dark shiny top out of a box and began to cut it up into thick slices. The water gathered in Aggie's mouth as she watched with fascinated eyes, the slices roll off the knife and felt the rich gingery smell reach her nose.

At last Mrs McClurg stopped cutting and when she heard Katy heave a carefully guarded sigh and lean back again in her chair, Aggie knew her sister had counted the slices and was satisfied with the result.

'There now! I'll brew the tea and then we'll wait for the men,' Mrs McClurg said, 'and how's your Auntie Lizzie?'

'Fine, thank you!' Aggie answered, wondering if she should mention Jamie Watson at all.

'I hear Wallie Johnstone has given up the poaching. He has found a new love!' Mrs McClurg said as she sat down and looked at Aggie to see how far her understanding of such things went, 'and it's your Auntie Lizzie!' she added.

Aggie swallowed and nodded. 'Ma knows he likes Auntie Lizzie, but we all thought he liked poaching better,' she answered uncertainly.

'Well, he doesn't now! He says it's time he got settled and he's going to take the chance with Jamie Watson out of the way,' Mrs McClurg told her firmly. 'He always had a strong notion for your Auntie Lizzie! And she could do worse, for he's a fine set up man with his own bit of ground to him!'

'Yes, Mrs McClurg,' Aggie agreed politely.

'I favour Wallie, myself,' continued Mrs McClurg. 'Jamie's a very nice man but a woman can't wait forever. And Wallie will not keep her waiting long, I can tell you. Oh, here's your Da and Roderick! I'll pour the tea.'

When the men came in Katy asked Da about the little pig.

'It's outside in the sack,' he replied. 'It's a fine wee fellow, with a black spot on his side!'

They all sat in at the table and when Mrs McClurg had poured the tea, she told them to help themselves just as though they were at home. Gradually the scones and cheese and honey disappeared and lastly the gingerbread, which tasted every bit as good as it looked.

As Mrs McClurg and Roderick chatted with Da, Aggie looked round the room and caught sight of the two dressed dolls fastened to the walls, that had belonged to Bessie and Mary McClurg when they were little girls. They were barely grown up when they both died of the Big Flu the same week.

It must have been terribly quiet in the house after the girls had gone, Aggie thought. It must have been like losing somebody in a dark wood and never finding them again.

Over on the dresser stood the photographs of the two girls, with that of Ritchie Anderson, the Australian soldier, between them. Aggie had known Ritchie too, and had helped him to meet Mary McClurg that day he first fell in love with her.

Ritchie had been on leave from the front and had come to spend it with Miss Blackwell, as she and her brother had known his parents in the years gone by before they had emigrated.

It was a fine hay-day in early July and Aggie was peering through the spars of the gate at the workers in the hayfield close by—mostly women for the men were nearly all away. She became aware of somebody standing beside her and, looking sideways, she saw a pair of brown boots, and higher up a khaki uniform, and above that a hat turned up at the side. She knew at once who it was, for Ma had seen him when she was up at the byre, and had told them all about him.

Aggie's first instinct was to run back home, just across the lane, but the soldier stopped her.

'You're not afraid of me, little girl, eh?' he said and he spoke the same as the children from England, who had come to the town to be away from the air raids. Aggie, who was very young, hung her head. 'No, sir,' she answered timidly.

'And I can look over the same gate as you?' he asked.

'Yes, sir,' she almost whispered.

'That's better!' he replied, giving one of her long plaits a light tug.

Just then Mary McClurg had come round from behind a haystack with a rake in her hand, her long dark plaits wound round her head like a crown, her white teeth gleaming against her sunburnt face.

'Holy Jiminy!' exclaimed the Australian soldier.

Aggie had heard of the names of many saints and holy men, but that was one that she had never heard yet.

'Beg pardon, sir?' she inquired, her curiosity overcoming her shyness.

'I said Holy Jiminy!' he repeated. 'And don't call me "sir"! I'm just plain Ritchie Anderson, private, from a sheep farm in Australia. And now who's that?'

Aggie looked up at the lean brown face underneath the hat, to see who he meant.

'Oh,' she cried out, 'that's Grannie Creedie!' thinking he was looking at the elderly figure in the sunbonnet.

'Never,' he argued, 'that's nobody's grannie! Not with black hair and—'

'Oh, you mean Mary McClurg!' Aggie laughed, her shyness gone. 'That's Bessie McClurg's sister.'

'Mary McClurg. Mary McClurg,' Ritchie repeated to himself. 'And what's your name?' he asked, suddenly looking down at her.

'Aggie,' she answered simply.

'Well Aggie, do you know Mary McClurg to speak to?'

'I've known her all my life,' Aggie told him solemnly, 'and Bessie too. Bessie is eighteen. Mary is seventeen. I'm eight this month!'

'Aggie, do you think you could go and talk to Mary McClurg and let me come along with you?' Ritchie asked.

'Ma gets cross if I go into the hayfield,' Aggie answered doubtfully.

'But Ma will not get cross with me!' laughed the soldier. 'Aggie, my leave only lasts ten days, I may never have another one. But you wouldn't know what that means!'

Aggie in her childishness could only grasp half of what the soldier was saying and she did not understand at the time why he did not go and speak to Mary McClurg himself. But maybe he was backward and shy like herself, she thought.

'I'll open the gate and you slip through in front of me,' insisted Ritchie undoing the hasps.

And then Aggie had an idea that came like a flash. It was one of the brightest ideas she had ever had in her life and it surprised herself.

'I'll ask Mary if she would like a drink of water! You can carry the can!' she said to Ritchie with some excitement. 'There it is at the hedge!'

'Aggie,' said the soldier as he picked it up, 'if you had been Commander in Chief of the Allied Armies, the war would be won, and over and done with, long before now!'

Aggie led the way across the clover. She had to watch out where she stepped for she was in her bare feet.

'Mary,' she said to the young girl with the long wooden rake in her hands, 'the soldier brought you a drink of water!'

The girl looked up and her eyes met those of the young man. No word was spoken as he handed her the can. She drank from the side and handed it back. Then Ritchie did a queer thing. He turned the can round and drank from where Mary's lips had been. A pink blush spread over the girl's face and she looked down at the ground.

'Agnes,' Ma's voice came from the cottage door. 'Come out of the hayfield at once!' Aggie turned and ran back to the gate.

So Ritchie Anderson courted Mary McClurg and returned on his next leave to continue the courtship. He bought her a diamond ring and said they were engaged, although Roderick thought his daughter was too young.

Then the war was over and Ritchie sailed for Australia in the troopship with Mary's promise that she would come out to marry him in a few months' time. The Big Flu reached the Little Valley and carried Bessie and Mary McClurg, as well as many others, to another land.

Aggie was still staring at the portraits when she felt Katy pushing her arm. 'Aggie, Mrs McClurg's speaking to you!' she was saying.

Aggie felt herself blushing.

'I was just telling your Da,' Mrs McClurg said in a soft kind of voice, as though she guessed where the girl's thoughts had been, 'that we had a Christmas card and a long letter from Ritchie and his folks!'

'That was nice!' Aggie answered, choking a little and those old friends, her tears, threatened to rise again.

'They said, 'continued Mrs McClurg firmly, 'that Ritchie hopes to visit us all again some day and that it was their summertime now. Fancy that!'

The matter-of-fact statement restored Aggie's balance for she remembered learning that in her geography lesson at the school.

'I'll be thankful when it's our summertime,' Roddie said, as if he wanted to end a painful subject. 'Let's hope it will be as good a one as the last one.'

'Aye, that you never can tell,' Da answered as he got up. 'I think we'd better be making for home. The days are beginning to lengthen a little, but it soon gets dark for all that.'

'So it does,' agreed Mrs McClurg. 'I hope, though, you'll be back soon.'

'Oh yes. She'll be along herself when the clear nights come in, I was to tell you,' Da replied.

'That'll be just fine, David,' she said going to the door with them. 'I'll look forward to seeing ye all soon then.'

'Aye, don't leave it too long till your next visit,' confirmed Roddie, 'and I hope the pig does extra well with ye, David.'

'Thank you, Roddie. And you too, Mrs McClurg.'

The little pig was squealing lustily in the sack that Aggie and Da carried between them. At the top of the hill they turned to wave to the McClurg's, standing at the cottage door, then they made their way down the brae like a small procession.

'Da, the rabbits will have a fine time now,' Katy cried from the back.

'How's that?' he asked.

'Wallie isn't going to poach any more. He's going to court Auntie Lizzie instead, Mrs McClurg says, and he'll not keep her waiting either!'

'Oh, I don't think Wallie will stay away from the poaching for long,' Da replied, and there was a trace of laughter in his voice. 'But we'll see. Have you got Janey's hand?'

'Yes, Da.'

Aggie looked over the darkening valley, where the lights of the town were beginning to twinkle in the distance.

Jamie Watson's clear kind face rose before her mind and then Wallie's dark one, so full of secrets. It was like the Gow Burn and the river. You could never compare the two, but you knew which was the safer.

'Aggie,' Janey called out. 'I heard Roddie say today that the crows start building their nests on the first Sunday in March.'

'Oh?'

'Aggie?'

'Mm?'

'How do the crows know when it's the first Sunday in March? Who tells them?'

There was a minute's silence as Aggie racked her brains for an answer.

'They'll see it in the paper, very likely!' Da said at last.

'Oh!' and Janey was satisfied.

Chapter Ten

THE coming of the spring in the South-West was like the tide coming up the river for no matter how strong was the down-current, the tide always won.

So it was with the spring. The sudden frosts, the showers of snow and the storms of sleet, that came again and again, retreated slowly but surely before the soft wind that would steal up from the bay. March borrowed a few days of summer and April would take a few from winter, as the seasons always did in the Little Valley.

The snowdrops stayed their short time then faded and the crocuses and daffodils were beginning to bloom in Miss Blackwell's orchard. The smell in the morning was green, with a rustling of dead leaves at the bottom of the hedges, and the faint sobbing hiss of grass and green shoots thrusting their way into the light.

Aggie listened to the chorus of birds in the early morning and watched the geese fly north from the bay. The pair of Craigie herons that nestled each year in the Castle Wood flew back low along the windings of the river to their old haunt with an unhurried beat of wings, for they knew where they were going.

Da began to talk of sowing the corn. 'I need a good dry day, with just the right wind,' he said.

When Da stepped over the ground and threw the handfuls of seed crossways, to one side and then to the other, from the shallow tray of corn hung round his neck, Aggie always thought of the china plate that decorated Grandma Breen's wall. It had a pink rim with a gold edge and in the middle was the painting of a man stepping over the brown earth and casting the seed just like Da in the sowing time.

Granda Breen always liked to be told when the corn was sown, for he used to say that he would live to see it harvested.

'There's no fear of anything happening to you that quick,' Grandma insisted. 'You have more ill to do yet!'

At this Granda chuckled, for it gave him a fine little air of devilry.

The hardest thing to believe was that Wallie Johnstone had given up poaching, and was taking his courting seriously. When Auntie Lizzie paid her visits to the house, he now arrived to escort her home, dressed in his best blue suit and wearing a felt hat.

The way he wore the hat, pulled down just a little to one side, gave him a handsome jaunty air, and Aggie was forced to admit to Katy that he was good to look at.

'So he is!' affirmed Katy, 'specially when he flashes his teeth!'

'But you heard what Granda said yesterday,' Aggie reminded her sister.

'I did. That it was easy to give up poaching in the spring, when there was nothing worth poaching. But Granda forgot about the salmon!'

'I expect he did,' replied Aggie.

'Anyway it was Jamie Watson's own fault!' Katy rattled on. 'He just should have got christened!'

'Maybe he should,' thought Aggie, 'but it's not the same any more.'

Aggie's mind was full of much thought these days on the

way to and from the school, for as well as Jamie Watson's romantic setbacks, there was the Qualifying not far away, just like a hoodie crow sitting on the roof. As far as Jamie Watson was concerned she could do nothing but feel sorry for him, and wish that things would come right between him and Auntie Lizzie. 'I think it's only in the papers that folks' love affairs end happily ever after,' she told herself. 'Ritchie's and Mary McClurg's didn't! And now look at Auntie Lizzie and Jamie!'

'Aggie!' Janey, who was reciting her multiplication tables at the back, called out. 'What's nine times seven?'

'Sixty-three!' Aggie answered and realized she ought to go over the weights and measures that Mrs McMinn had given her to do.

With the lengthening of the days, however, Aggie was able to go and meet Ma coming from the milking in the evenings after Da arrived home. This night she was waiting at the byre door when a man from the town garage drove a new shiny little motor-car into the farmyard and asked for Miss Blackwell. A few minutes later Aggie grasped the fact that this was a motor-car that Miss Blackwell had ordered for herself, unknown to her brother, who took another full minute to close his mouth, such was his astonishment.

'You once said you liked nothing better than surprises, Andrew,' she reminded him with much satisfaction. 'Well, here's one!'

'But, Jessie,' he turned to her and spoke as one would to a small child, 'you don't know how to drive it! It doesn't go by itself!'

'Were you born riding a bicycle?' she retorted.

'Of course not. I had to learn!'

'Very well,' replied his sister tartly. 'I can learn to drive this!'

'But this—this is different!' Andrew argued, his voice still thick with bewilderment. 'You're wasting your money. A bicycle is about all you need. You're never away anywhere!'

Miss Blackwell set down the two pails of milk she was

144

about to carry to the dairy and faced her brother, unmindful of either Aggie or the young man, for Ma was still inside the byre.

'That's just it, Andrew Blackwell: I *am* never anywhere! My bad leg keeps me from walking far and the bicycle doesn't help it any; and I'm just plain tired of being tied in so much,' she said in a firm, quiet voice.

'But Jessie, a woman's place is in! In the house—I mean!' he faltered.

'Andrew Blackwell!' she shouted back, and Aggie saw his eyes open wide in alarm. 'You're an old-fashioned stick-in-the-mud! You're quite content to see a woman work like a horse all day and maybe sit down at night—with the mending! You have all your joy-rides and your friends! You can have them for me, but when I learn to drive that motor-car, I can have something too! I'm still just a middle-aged woman, and I'd like to go to a concert in the town sometimes and visit my friends as well! And furthermore—'

'But Jessie,' he interrupted, 'I didn't mean—'

But Miss Blackwell was going to have her say and get it over.

'And furthermore,' she continued in a more peaceful tone, 'there's talk of a country woman's society being formed—the Rural something or other, and the meetings are being held in the Glen schoolhouse. That's a good four miles from here, but I intend to join and I'm inviting Mrs Kenny to go with me! So there! That's why I've bought a motor-car!' With that she stooped and picked up the milk-pails and made for the dairy with Andrew at her heels, the perplexed frown still on his face. The progress of woman was just too fast for him.

'Ma!' Aggie asked excitedly on the way home. 'Will you go with Miss Blackwell to the Glen schoolhouse?'

Ma's blue eyes were eager and shining, for she was now acquainted with the whole story.

'Oh, I'd like to very much! But we'll have to see what your Da says. He's a bit like Andrew Blackwell!'

Every evening after that, while it was still clear, Miss Blackwell went slowly up and down the lane in her motor-car with the young man from the garage, teaching her to drive.

Da said they were all to keep off the road at that time in case it made her nervous, and she might run into something.

Big Charlie showed no such respect for Miss Blackwell's feelings. At first he stared over the gate with great curiosity at the 'thing' moving slowly up and down the lane and then he trotted along with it. When Miss Blackwell's driving improved and she could move faster, he broke into a noisy gallop, and kicked up his heels with excitement. Da offered to shift him to another field. 'Indeed no, David,' she answered. 'If I can't learn to drive with a horse looking at me what will I do when I have to go through the town?'

When Miss Blackwell turned the car in front of the house, with them all watching from the window, John talked about the clutch and the carburettor and other words to do with engines, that he had heard about. Katy nodded her head in admiration, for she was keeping in with John for a particular reason. She hoped he would ask her to be his partner to the social and dance being held in the Village School to end the evening classes for that winter. When she heard that Robert was going with John, she was much put out.

'Mercy me, I never heard of such a thing!' Ma said in astonishment. 'Such things are for those left the school. What would you do there?'

'She'll be wanting to put her hair up next!' Da remarked from behind the paper, where he had taken refuge.

'Katy, you can't dance!' Janey pointed out to her. 'Only a wee bit of the Highland Fling!'

'Neither can Robert nor John!' Katy argued huffily.

'They'll learn to mix with company,' Ma replied, 'and next winter if there's a dancing class in the town, maybe they could both go to it, that is, if I can persuade Robert to go.'

But it took Katy a day or two to get over her disappointment.

The fields where Da had sown the corn were harrowed

and rolled and the first larks were singing high above the meadows when the great March winds began to blow. They cleared the valley of the last dead things of winter—the old leaves, the rotting limbs of trees, the dried canes of last year's reeds, the withered twigs. They swept the roads clean and sent great clouds of dust rolling along the lanes and the cart tracks.

On one such afternoon, Auntie Lizzie waited for the girls to come out of school, which was now four o'clock like the rest, to walk out home with them.

Out on the Big Road the strong wind from the north-west blew them along at almost a running pace and Aggie had to clutch Janey's hand tight for she saw that Auntie Lizzie had her own troubles. With one hand she had to hold down her long wide skirts and with the other keep her hat anchored safely on the top of her head.

'Goodness!' she panted, for the wind blew her breath away. 'This is terrible. I had no idea it was so blowy.'

'Auntie Lizzie, I can see your petticoat!' Katy suddenly shrilled.

'Oh, no!' and Auntie Lizzie clutched her skirt more tightly.

'There's nobody looking but us,' Katy tried to console her.

Hardly had she said this, than a man, pushing a bike, came out of the lane, which they were now approaching, his head bent into the wind.

Aggie could see Auntie Lizzie's skirts whirling up again as the gusts pulled at them and the white frill of her petticoat came into view once more. Then the wind gave another vicious tug and in an effort to save her modesty, Auntie Lizzie let go her hat and held on to her skirts with both hands.

The north-wester wasted no time. With a wrench, it jerked the hat joyously up into the air, then whirled it down on to the road, where it cartwheeled along until it struck a stone. Flattening out, it slithered to rest at the feet of the man pushing the bike.

Aggie could have laughed at the sudden surprised way the man stopped and stared at the hat, before he picked it up. But the laugh was quickly stifled when the man looked up with the hat in his hand and she saw it was Jamie Watson.

'Oh, just look at that!' she heard Auntie Lizzie say and her further remark was lost in the wind.

'I hope Katy minds what she says,' was Aggie's first thought and then she wondered just what she would say herself.

'Is this yours, Lizzie?' he asked as they came forward, which Aggie thought was a needless question, considering that he had seen the hat on Auntie Lizzie's head often enough.

'Thank you, Jamie,' she replied, still holding her skirts down and drawing into the shelter of the high thorn hedge that began here. 'As a matter of fact, it is mine.'

'It's a mighty strong wind,' Jamie then said, and this time looked at Aggie.

'It is that,' she agreed, and she thought what a nice face he had, with no tricks in it. 'Were you out at the house?'

'No, Aggie. I was doing a bit of work for Miss Blackwell.'

'Jamie, have you seen the new pig?' Janey asked. 'He fair likes his pig-house!'

'Does he, indeed!' Jamie laughed, tapping her on the head with Auntie Lizzie's hat' 'That's fine. I hope he does well in it.'

A silence fell then and Aggie saw Katy move over beside Auntie Lizzie, just to show she was sticking up for her, while the latter, still holding her skirts, was staring out over Jamie's head into the distance. Aggie wished that Jamie would turn round and look at her instead of at the front wheel of his bicycle, for the wind had made her very nice-looking. Her red-brown hair curled round her face like a frame, her cheeks were rosy, and her grey eyes, with the fine little wrinkles at the corners, were bright and clear

All of a sudden Auntie Lizzie broke the silence.

'We'd better be getting along now, Agnes! Your Ma will

be looking out for you,' she said in a tight kind of voice as she turned away.

'Oh, Lizzie!' Jamie called out.

'Yes,' she answered over her shoulder.

'Here's your hat,' he said.

'Thank you, Jamie,' and she clapped it straight on her head and marched off down the road.

'Come on, Katy,' Aggie said, 'we'd better catch up with Auntie Lizzie. Ta-ta, Jamie!' and she started to run. She heard Katy say something to Jamie and then run behind her and in a few minutes they were alongside Auntie Lizzie. 'He's a mean, stubborn man!' she was saying. 'Pig-headed, that's what he is! And he never once asked me how I was getting on!' and she gulped.

'But, Auntie Lizzie,' Aggie said timidly, 'maybe he was shy before us!'

'He's not that shy,' she replied.

'Auntie Lizzie!' Janey panted as she trotted behind, 'you're walking too quick!'

Suddenly Auntie Lizzie stopped. 'Oh, Janey. I'm a mean thing too!' she said, blowing her nose and wiping her eyes. 'How can I expect your little legs to keep up with my long strides! We'll stop a minute here, for this hedge is fine shelter.'

'Never mind, Auntie Lizzie,' Katy said with great sympathy, 'I told him that I, for one, didn't like his pig-house!'

'Oh Katy, you didn't!' Aggie exclaimed.

'I did so!' and the tassel on her tammy nodded vigorously.

Aggie looked back and was surprised to see that Jamie was still standing watching them. With a defiant look at Katy she waved and he waved back, and then turned on to the Big Road into the full force of the wind.

'Auntie Lizzie, Aggie waved!' Katy said in a shocked voice.

'Well!' replied Aggie boldly. 'Auntie Lizzie only said he was stubborn, she never said she didn't like him!'

'Agnes, you're coming on,' her aunt said looking at her curiously. 'He always liked you girls. He has known you all your days. It's just me he has stopped liking!'

As they covered their faces and waited for the next big dust cloud to whirl past, Aggie knew fine that that was not true, but again she never could manage to explain it.

However with the Qualifying drawing near, everybody's love affairs dwindled to a far corner of Aggie's mind. During the day Mrs McMinn's warnings, threats and sometimes praise took up all of Aggie's attention and the road to and from the school was too full of interest to allow any time for thinking.

The hedges were full of nests, some still in the early stages of building, and mostly belonging to hedge-sparrows, thrushes, or yellow-yoits. The blackbirds, Aggie noticed, favoured the whins, which were now beginning to bloom against the dike-side. In the Little Wood a yellow flower grew in the damp places and the leaves of the bluebells were all spread out, waiting for the flower stalk to rise up from the middle.

The spring days brought more people out on the roads. There were the tramps and the tinkers, a dark-haired, brown skinned people with many children, the beggars and the pedlars, some with goods to sell, like safety-pins, linen threads or boot-laces, some who mended pot lids or soldered kettles while-you-wait, some who made baskets out of willow wands or whittled clothes-pegs, and others who just begged. Aggie knew most of them, for they had been on the roads as far as she could think back, disappearing in winter, and coming out again as soon as the days got brighter. Everybody knew the old tramps were harmless, for most of them just could not bear to have anything but the open sky above them, but the tinkers were different. They stole anything they could lay hands on, hens, washing from the line, even horses, and thought nothing of laying a curse on a house where they did not get what they wanted.

When the threshing mill came round to the Farm, Ma's

thoughts turned to the cleaning, for there was plenty of clean, fresh chaff for the mattresses. For days after, Aggie could smell the strawy smell when she lay down to sleep. The kitchen dresser and chairs were given a new coat of mahogany varnish, but no wall-papering was being done this year as money was short since the pig died.

Aggie could see that Ma was looking forward to the summer and the extra money it always brought, for everybody needed something new in clothes. Just now she was saving to get John a new Sunday suit for his shoulders had broadened out so much that he hardly dared to move in his present one. Da was patching up his oilskin leggings to see him through the spring, everybody needed something new for their feet, and although Aggie's own coat had been let down at the cuffs and hem, it was still short.

And only Ma worried about these things, for the rest thought little about them. Nobody ever thought of Ma's clothes either. Aggie had seen her in the same navy costume on Sundays since she could remember, and over it in winter she wore a dark grey coat.

Someday, Aggie used to dream, when she was rich she would buy Ma a real fur coat like there was in the Catalogue. It would be nothing like the fur that Mrs McKay flung round her shoulders on Sundays, for that was just like the skin of some animal with a snout and a bushy tail. Robert said it was a fox.

'Do you think Mr McKay caught it when it was sneaking up to their henhouse?' Janey asked.

At this Robert laughed and said that the McKays had no henhouse, but Aggie always thought it a shameful end for any poor little wild animal.

March went out like a lion, leaving a fresh covering of snow on the top of Cairnsmore and a wintry chill in the air.

'It'll not last,' Da said. 'The wind's changing already!'

By the time April was a few days old, the wayward spring had softened its mood again, with the white crest on the top of the mountain as the last reminder of winter.

At home Da and the boys were digging up the garden and the flower borders, and trimming the path edges, for Da was a very tidy man. All this had to be done after the day's work was over, for only jobs that could not be done any other day were done on Sundays. The sabbath day was still the Lord's Day, whether folk went to church or not, and it was the only day that there was any rest after the hard toil of the week.

In other years Aggie raked the fields and the river bank with Robert and John on a Sunday afternoon if the day was at all dry, but of late she noticed that they were less inclined to go than they used to. She knew what was happening to them, for they were growing up, as she had seen it happen to others, and the delight of finding the primroses growing on the river bank and the nests in strange places was not enough any more.

But this Sunday early in April the boyish urge made itself felt again in her brothers, and Aggie got into her heavy boots and set off with them through the Far Orchard and into the fields beyond.

By and by they found themselves along the river close to the Castle. To Aggie the Castle was an eerie place for it was haunted. Everybody said a white lady walked there on moonlight nights and a carriage and pair, driven by a headless coachman, galloped up the drive, whenever a death took place in the laird's family.

The only sound to break the stillness as Aggie and her brothers peered from the other side of the fence through the rhododendron bushes, to the avenue, was the soft cooing of pigeons near the white wooden gates. Suddenly another sound reached their ears; someone was marching briskly up the avenue.

'Robert, come on home!' Aggie whispered, terrified of what she might see.

'Ssh!' hushed her brother. 'It's the laird himself!'

A short elderly figure in a tweed knickerbocker suit and a deerstalker came into view, with a garden broom on his shoulder, and stood to attention just opposite the bush which hid them. For the next five minutes they watched the laird putting himself through a sharp and silent course of army drill, with the broom for a rifle, and when it was over he turned and marched smartly back down the avenue out of sight.

At first they were too surprised to say anything and nobody would dare laugh at the laird.

'He used to be a soldier, they say,' Robert said at last as they stole back into the open fields.

'If he had caught us watching him you know what would have happened!' John exclaimed.

'What?' asked Aggie.

'He would have shot us with the broom handle!'

At this they laughed so much that the water came to Aggie's eyes and she failed to see the gamekeeper come from behind the clump of thorns until he was on them.

'Nice mild day!' he greeted them, 'but it'll likely rain before night. The clouds are low and the whaups are whistling. Having your Sunday walk?'

'Ay,' Robert answered, 'we often go round the fields.'

'I know that, boy,' the keeper said kindly. 'I've seen you many a time. It's not often I go out on a Sunday, but I just thought I'd take a walk round the policies myself!'

'Any poaching going on, Mr Malcolm?' John asked. Aggie knew John asked this for sheer curiosity for there was always poaching going on.

'Some. But not as much as there used to be!' the keeper answered with a sly laugh. 'I'm just wondering how long it will last!'

They all knew he was meaning Wallie Johnstone.

Chapter Eleven

THE day of the Qualifying was a Saturday and the sun
came up a little late for Cairnsmore wore his misty cap
and some grey clouds were loitering about in the sky. A
light wind rose up from the west and the clouds drifted away
like smoke, leaving wide patches of blue. There was all the
promise of a fine cool April day, with perhaps a shower or
two and a rainbow straddling the hills.

Da had called Aggie early as usual and before he left the
house had dallied for a moment at the door.

'Mind the fire, Agnes,' he warned her like he always did,
and then clearing his throat, added a little awkwardly, 'Do
your best at the examination, Agnes. It's not everybody gets
the chance!'

Again he hesitated. 'Will you be walking into the town
by yourself?'

'Yes, Da. Ma thinks Katy needs a rest on a Saturday.'

'Well, don't be speaking to anybody you don't know.
You never can tell with strangers. Ta-ta.'

'Na-poo, Aggie!' the boys called out, and that was their
way of wishing her well.

'I can hardly believe it's today,' she thought to herself,

watching her father stride up the lane. 'I seem to have heard nothing but Qualifying for months now!'

Yesterday Mrs McMinn had gone over most of the points with the class, then she had lectured the school again on the value of education, with a few last warnings. 'The examination takes place, as you know, in the Big School. The morning session starts at ten o'clock sharp. Be there in plenty of time, bringing with you only a pen, a ruler and a pencil. The afternoon session begins at two o'clock and ends at three-thirty. Read each question over several times and think carefully before you put down your answer. When it comes to your composition, choose the subject about which you know the most. Now do your best, all of you, and may God's grace be with you!'

It was a solemn moment and Aggie understood just how Mrs McMinn felt, for the success or failure of her pupils would reflect on her too.

'Are you wearing your best frock, Aggie?' Cathie Gemmell wanted to know later. 'You'll not be coming in your big boots surely!'

Aggie reddened. She had no best frock yet, but only the jumper she wore on Sunday over her week-day skirt, which Ma would press at night.

'It's not what you've got on that counts,' said Eddie Campbell, who was listening as usual. 'Aggie's brains are in her head anyway, not in her feet like some folks. Ha! Ha!' he bellowed.

'Nobody asked you,' Cathie retorted huffily.

'Bah!' was Eddie's reply as his tongue shot out.

'Come on, Cathie.' Helen McKay linked her arm in her friend's. 'When we go to the High School we won't have to speak to the likes of him!'

'You have to get in first!' Eddie snickered.

Aggie managed to escape further questions and was glad when she was safely out on the Big Road. It was all right for Cathie Gemmell to talk of best frocks, she was the only one in her family. Aggie looked sideways at Katy, kicking up little clouds of dust with her boots, her straight fair hair just like her own, pulled back from her smallish freckled face and swinging in two long plaits behind her.

'Aggie!' Janey called in an excited voice. 'There's a Red Admiral!'

'So it is!' Katy stopped to look at the dancing butterfly. 'It's out too early. Did you see it, Aggie?'

Aggie nodded and hung her head. She would not be Cathie Gemmell for a hundred best frocks, walking by herself, sleeping by herself, with nobody to show things to.

'Aggie,' Katy asked anxiously, 'does your back shiver when you think about tomorrow? Do you have things running up and down?'

Aggie wished she could throw back her head and say carelessly, 'I have not,' but she was used to telling the truth. 'A bit,' she admitted. 'I don't know anybody from the Big School and Cathie Gemmell and Helen McKay both do. But Ma says I can wear my button boots.'

'That won't be so bad,' answered Katy, who thought heavy boots were the worst thing that could happen to anybody. 'It's terrible when you trip and everybody sees the tackets!'

'What would make Aggie trip?' Janey asked.

'Everybody can trip.' Katy turned such a severe face on her young sister that it silenced her.

So now it was the Day and there was Ma coming down the lane from the byre. High up above the hayfield a lark was singing and a feeling of envy passed through Aggie when she heard it. Ah well, she was no lark, but a shy and gawky country girl, going to sit the first examination of her life in the town, and the birds of the air had no such things to worry about.

'Your jumper and skirt look very nice, Agnes,' Ma greeted her, watching the swinging pleats with great satisfaction, 'and it's going to be a fine day!'

'Aggie,' Katy called from the bedroom, 'don't go till we're up!'

'Oh, there's plenty of time yet! It's only half-past seven and I won't be leaving till nearly nine!'

When Aggie said that, she believed that the time to leave was still a long way off, but after breakfast was over and Ma had plaited her hair so that the new blue ribbons would not slip off, and the hens and pig were fed, she looked up at the clock in surprise.

'Ay,' Ma said. 'It's coming on. You'd better get ready now, Agnes, so that you're there in plenty of time.'

A little hammer of excitement began to thump inside her as she got down her coat, with Katy and Janey watching her in silence.

'I know you'll do all you can, Agnes,' Ma said, following her to the door. 'We'll all be thinking about you, the whole of the day. Be careful on the road and come straight home.'

'Yes Ma, so I will.'

'Have you everything with you?'

'Yes, Ma. A pen, a pencil and a ruler, and a clean hankie,' Aggie answered and she had a queer unreal feeling as though it was another Aggie who was speaking and turning to wave as she went off up the lane.

The feeling passed and she looked back through a blur of tears before she reached the Rosy Hollow. 'I'll do my very best,' she said to herself with lips that trembled, when they were out of sight. 'I'll try my hardest so that Ma will not be disappointed in me.'

She was glad for once that there was no sign of Miss Blackwell at the farm, for her eyes were red. Round the bend stretched the lonely road with the first white stars of Bethlehem beginning to show in the grass along the bottom of the budding hedge and the whins bright yellow against the dike side. The birds twittered and sang and Aggie, taking a moment to peep into a blackbird's nest, met the beady eye of the hen sitting on her eggs.

She was relieved that no one was in sight for she liked the road to herself, and when she reached the end of the lane, she stood and listened for anything that might be

F   157

coming along the Big Road. She only did this when she was alone, for once during last year's summer holidays, she was on her way into the town and was just leaving the lane when a huge grey animal loomed into sight along the Big Road.

Aggie lost no time getting over the dike and when her first fear had passed, had looked through a space between the stones. 'That's an elephant!' she breathed to herself in wonderment. 'I'm sure that's an elephant! It's just the same as the picture in the Wild Animal book at the school. My goodness!'

Walking beside it was a dark-skinned man in white clothes and a white thing on his head. Behind the elephant came a stream of horse-drawn wagons, all painted in bright colours and when everything had passed and she stood on the top of the dike to see the last of that great animal, she guessed she had seen a circus moving on to the next town.

Later Nathan Thomson had said it was a good thing that the lions and tigers inside the wagons—for they were certainly there, as it was no circus without them—had not got her scent. 'They would have roared in anger and burst their cages and ate you up!' he told her. Robert and John had laughed at this when they heard it, but Katy and Janey both agreed that she had had a narrow escape.

Near the town Aggie met the grocer, perched high on his van, with his old brown horse trotting peacefully along. 'Fine day, Agnes!' he greeted her, with a twirl of his whip. 'You're going the wrong way!' for the grocer liked company and most Saturdays he had one or two of the town boys along with him.

When she reached the policeman's corner, the town clock on the other side of the bridge struck a quarter to ten, and five more minutes took her to the Big School. There were groups of boys scattered about in the playground and when she found her way to the girls' cloakroom, it was filled with a chattering throng of girls.

From a far corner, Cathie Gemmell waved to her. Aggie

knew Cathie well enough not to expect her to come and speak to her, for Cathie thought herself far above a ploughman's daughter, if there happened to be anybody else about. So Aggie took her time about hanging up her coat and taking her handkerchief out of her pocket, putting it up her sleeve, and then pretending she had left something else in her other pocket. Then a gentleman with a shiny bald head opened the schoolroom door and suggested that they all go in and take their places. 'A pen, a pencil, and a ruler are all that you are allowed to take into the examination room,' he announced.

So Aggie went in to face the problems. The day of the Qualifying was one in which she made many discoveries. The silence of the examination room, broken only by the rustle of paper, the scraping of pens, and an occasional sigh from some baffled candidate, was a new experience for her. The easy-looking questions often had a catch to them, while the difficult looking ones needed some simple sorting out. She tried to keep to Mrs McMinn's advice about reading each question over several times, and not rushing to put down the answer. Then a glance at the clock on the wall made her panic in case she would not be able to complete the paper in the given time, and she had to control that too.

During the morning break and at dinner-time, everybody groaned and said it was all terrible and started to compare the answers. Sometimes Aggie's results agreed and sometimes not, and her spirits rose and then sank so often that it was a great relief to reach Granda's for her dinner.

'And how are you getting on?' Grandma asked.

For a moment Aggie hesitated. 'I think I'm getting on all right,' she answered, feeling less confident than she sounded. 'Is Auntie Lizzie in?'

'No, she's along at Alice Robinson's helping her to paper the kitchen.'

'Your Auntie Lizzie's never in her own house!' roared Granda.

'Go on with you,' Grandma replied. 'That's not true. She only goes out to Agnes' mother and the church. She's a good daughter.'

'I know she's a good daughter,' he shouted back. 'But she can only think of marrying a heathen or a poacher. How's that with the country full of fine men?'

'I've been in this world over seventy years and the fine men are few and far between,' Grandma laughed. 'There's a plate of good thick broth, Agnes. Do the other boys and girls speak to you?'

'Yes, Grandma!' Aggie answered. 'At the morning break we were all talking together and now at dinner-time too!'

Aggie left out the fact that she had gone through some tormented moments when some of the girls first spoke to her and she could only answer 'yes' and 'no'. When one said she knew she was Agnes Kenny, and her parents were acquainted with Mr and Miss Blackwell, then Aggie managed to give a sensible answer that led to a discussion about the arithmetic paper with several others joining in.

Then she had discovered she was the only girl in buttoned boots and she imagined that several of the girls were looking at her feet with great curiosity.

'It's good for you to meet new faces,' Grandma said. 'You don't get a chance of mixing with folks living away out there. It makes you tongue-tied!'

Again Aggie kept her thoughts to herself for she would not have disagreed with Grandma for worlds, only Grandma could not understand how glad she was to get back 'out there' with no new faces to bother with.

'If you get by this—this—whatever it is,' Granda shouted, 'you'll get a leather case for your books from me, mind that! I see the rest of the High School lassies have got them!'

'I'd like that,' she blushed. 'Thank you Granda!'—Aggie was much surprised that he should notice what the High School girls carried their books in!

'I don't miss much even though I am coming seventy-five!'

he yelled at her then, as though reading her thoughts, 'though it doesn't seem that long since I was your age!'

Grandma smoothed her apron and sighed gently. 'That's true, Agnes,' she agreed. 'A lifetime goes by like a whiff of wind. However, there's nothing a body can do to alter it!' and she smiled brightly again as she asked, 'What do you get this afternoon?'

'English,' replied Aggie. 'Composition that is. Mrs McMinn says I'm better at that than at sums.'

'Oh, well, you can but do your best.'

Back at her desk in the examination room Aggie studied the choice of essays. She knew she ought to pick one that had something to do with nature, for that was certainly the subject about which she knew the most.

'I'll take the one called 'Spring', she thought to herself, 'since we're in the middle of it!'

Looking at the sunny sky through the school window, she dipped the pen in the inkwell, thought for a moment or two and then started off. She put down all she knew, from the bursting stillness of a February night, the geese leaving the bay, the morning frosts, the warming midday sun, the cold bite of a north wind that shamefully swung round to the south and the soft rain, the nesting birds, the daffodils already deep in grass, the green spikes of the reeds along the river, and the young corn, to the larks, singing as high as they could soar in the sky above the Little Valley.

And then she could write no more. Looking up at the round-faced clock she saw it was twenty-past three and at the same time, the bald-headed man, who had been seated at the desk out in front all day, got up and strolled quietly to and fro.

A little wave of movement swept through the room, although a few pens were still scraping on and one boy was chewing savagely on the end of his penholder as he read over his work. Then the clock struck half-past three and everybody was asked to blot their papers well and hand them in.

'Well, that's the Qualifying done with!' one girl said to

Agnes as they trooped back to the cloakroom. 'Thank goodness, we get our Easter holidays next week. I just hope we all pass!'

'Just think' said the girl who had first talked to Aggie in the morning, 'if we all pass, we'll all be in the same class. That'll be fine, eh Agnes?'

'Yes, I too hope it's like that,' answer Aggie politely, wishing she could speak in that free and easy manner that the town girls could manage so well.

'Grandma was right again!' she thought as she left the town, which was full of folk since it was Saturday afternoon. 'I am tongue-tied! Katy and John aren't. They're shy, too, but not so bad as Robert and me.'

For years Robert's shyness had annoyed Ma for he used to hide over at the river bank when visitors came, and only came back after they had gone. That was all over now and he went among folk like anybody else, although Aggie knew he was still a quiet one, liking his own company.

She kept close to the Big Wall when she heard the smart clip-clop of a pony and machine behind her. The horse slowed down when it came abreast and Hughie Grant, the milk-tester, hailed her from his high seat.

'Come on aboard, Agnes!' he called out. 'I'm spending the week-end with Miss Blackwell. My, this is a grand spring day,' he added, as he grasped her hand and helped her up from the step into the seat beside him. 'Weather like this will soon melt the last of the snow on old Cairnsmore there!'

Aggie smiled in delighted agreement for she had known Hughie Grant long enough for the early shyness to be worn off. 'It's nice to be out on a day like this,' she answered.

'It's nice to be young in the springtime, Agnes,' he said back. 'Gee-up, Nancy!

> Land o'silvery winding Cree
> Land o' fell and forest free-ee.
> Land that's ay sae dear tae me-ee,
> Bonnie Gallowa,'

he sang loudly and the pony frisked into a playful gallop.

'Canny there, Nancy! I'm singing to Agnes!'

Aggie laughed and looked round her, for there was a fine view from the seat beside the milk-tester. She could see the smooth green fields on the other side of the Big Wall and the chestnut trees in the wood, bursting into leaf, and holding each twig curved upward like a candlestick for the white flower when it bloomed, and in the field beyond the high thorn hedge, the young corn was bright and green.

Leaning back a little she tried to look sideways at the milk-tester's bare head. His brown hair *did* grow in waves with the ends turning up in little curls, just as Katy said. 'I wish my hair was like that,' she thought to herself, remembering her own thick straight locks.

'How's your Auntie Lizzie?' the tester asked as they swung into the lane. He always inquired after her and if she happened to be at the house when he was staying at the Big Farm, he made a point of taking a walk down the lane so that he might have a chance of speaking to her. Ma was never very sure of this, as he was engaged to a girl up in Ayrshire, but Da said he was just a man who liked a bonny face, with no harm to him.

'Auntie Lizzie's fine,' Aggie replied. 'But she doesn't go with Jamie any more. Wallie's courting her now.'

'Mercy, I thought that tiff was patched up long ago,' the tester answered, bringing Nancy to a walk. 'You'll not have heard what happened to Jamie this morning then?'

'No, what happened?'

'He was fixing gates up at the Vennan Farm when he saw the bull turn on the byreman. He raced out with a stick to draw the bull's attention and of course it turned on him.'

'Oh!' Aggie was horrified as a terrible vision of Jamie being gored on the sharp horns of the bull rose before her. 'He's not dead, is he, Hughie?' The fearful words slipped out along with the milk-tester's first name, for they always called him Mr Grant to his face and only Hughie behind his back.

'No,' the other replied gravely, not noticing anything

wrong with his name. 'But he's been taken away to the Infirmary.'

'The Infirmary?'

'Yes. They'll soon find out there if he's badly hurt or not.'

'Auntie Lizzie will be in a state. I know fine she doesn't like Wallie half as much as she likes Jamie. We don't either.'

'We!' Who's we?' asked the tester curiously, turning his good-looking face to her.

'Katy and Janey and me.'

'Oh,' he paused. 'I like Jamie too. Wallie's not a bad fellow, mind you, but I don't think he's cut out for marrying.'

'Oh, poor Jamie!' Aggie sighed again.

'Mm. That's a bad bull up there at the Vennan. He'll kill somebody yet.'

'I wonder if Auntie Lizzie will go to see Jamie in the Infirmary,' Aggie said.

'If you like somebody enough, you'll run miles to see them!' the tester answered with a laugh. 'Giddup, Nancy, I have to get some tea before they start the milking.'

Passing under the trees of the Little Wood where the branches of the beeches nearly caught in her hair, Aggie wondered if Hughie Grant had been reading the story in the paper too, for he seemed to know the right thing to say. When she arrived home Da and the boys were already there, it being Saturday and early stopping, and everybody was seated round the table eating porridge. When Aggie told her news of Jamie Watson lying in the Infirmary, they all looked at her with great interest and the Qualifying was forgotten.

'Jamie's a man that never thinks of himself,' Da said, wiping his moustache, 'and it's time he did! Not that I think that he did wrong helping the other man, I don't mean that at all. But Jamie's far too soft-hearted and kind for his own good.'

Aggie could see that everybody was surprised, for Da very seldom uttered his opinions at such length.

'There's something in what you say,' Ma agreed. 'What's annoying me is that he has no family to visit him in the Infirmary and tomorrow, being Sunday, there's not a train to take any of us down.'

'Well, when I go into the town tonight, I'll ask the Doctor how he is and maybe he'll phone the Infirmary. It's the least we can do for a friend.'

'Can you not phone yourself?' Ma asked.

'How can I do that!' Da answered, getting up from the table. 'I've never handled such an instrument in all my days. Get ready boys, if you're coming.'

'How did you get on, Agnes?' Ma asked, and everybody waited for her answer.

'Fine, Ma. The other girls were nice and some of them spoke to me.'

'And the examination? Did ye manage it?'

'Well, I got the same answers as the rest in most things,' was all Aggie could think of replying.

'Oh then,' Da said, standing on a chair to get his best boots down from the shelf above the door, 'you can only do what you're fit to do. Look after your sisters when your ma leaves for the byre, for I'd better get on into the town.'

Later that night in bed, Aggie lay thinking over the happenings of the day. Several times Katy and Janey had asked her to tell them all about the Qualifying and the girls she met there.

'So the High School will not be so bad after all,' Katy had remarked, 'since you know some of them already.'

Ma had listened to all this very seriously as she went through their hair with the fine-tooth comb. Ma's thoughts were divided, Aggie could see that, for she was anxious about Jamie Watson and also about the Qualifying.

'I'm not much help to you there, Agnes,' she had said, 'because I had very little schoolin'. I hope you make the most of yours, the three of you.'

Lying in the dark, the memory of Ma's humble way of saying that, brought a lump to her throat, and the tears followed right away. She let them flow unhindered on to the calico pillow-slip for Katy and Janey were both asleep, and she could sniff as much as she wanted. She heard the very soft wind of early summer hush through the high hedge and then Da and the boys arrived home and there was only the murmur of their voices.

'I wish I could stop this greetin',' she said at last to herself. 'I never used to greet like this.' Somehow she felt better after that, and the heaviness left her. 'Maybe I did better in the Qualifying than I think. Maybe Jamie is not as badly hurt as I imagine,' she thought to herself, feeling lighter every minute, 'and next week we get our Easter holidays, and surely the teacher will not give us homework now.'

She remembered a picture she had seen of the inside of a hospital. It was all white and clean and everywhere there were smiling nurses. She drifted off into a peaceful sleep with the vision of a beautiful nurse propping Jamie up in his bed.

Chapter Twelve

NEXT morning Aggie wakened early for the long days were coming in and the daylight filtered into the room through the blind. Getting up quietly, so as not to disturb Katy or Janey, she dressed quickly and went along to the kitchen where Da had just come in from the stables.

Already the frying pan was hanging on the cleek over the fire and he was filling it with pieces of bacon for the breakfast. Plenty of men would have thought such tasks beneath them and would have waited for their wives to come home, but Aggie knew Da was not like that. If there was something to do he did it, although he never interfered with Ma's affairs in the house.

When Aggie asked him about Jamie Watson he said the news was not so bad as was supposed.

'The doctor was very civil. He said Jamie would be in the Infirmary for a week or two, but there's nothing broken.'

Aggie nodded with relief as she went to fetch rain-water out of the barrel at the corner of the house for her hands and face, for although the doctor never failed to answer a sick call, no matter the weather or the time of day or night, his temper was unpredictable. On one occasion when Robert was younger, he had been howling so much with the tooth-ache that Da had taken him in to the doctor late at night to have it pulled. The doctor had given them both a sound swearing, yanked the tooth out there and then, and shoved them both outside all in a matter of five minutes—although next morning he had called at the house to see if Robert had suffered any after-effects. Everybody said there was not much that the doctor did not know about folk—and especially those who lived in the Little Valley.

Just then Ma came in from the milking with more exciting news. 'Miss Blackwell says she'll drive you down to the Infirmary, Da, and Hughie Grant will go too,' she announced. 'It seems that the milk-tester can drive a car as well, and he'll take his turn.'

The excitement in the house was tremendous for it was a journey of more than a hundred miles altogether there and back. Aggie shined up Da's boots, Katy brushed his Sunday suit, and Robert and John saw to the pig and the hens and promised to give a hand in the byre and do the horses that evening.

'Jamie will get a fine surprise,' Ma said as she made up a little parcel of eggs, butter, and home-made jam. 'I suppose Lizzie will have her own thoughts about it all.'

'She has that,' replied Da firmly. 'I don't like to repeat this, but last night in her own house in front of her mother and father, she said that since Jamie was not badly hurt, he would have plenty of time to go over his shortcomings.'

'My goodness!' Ma exclaimed, plainly astonished. 'It seems that Lizzie has a hard side to her too!'

'So she will,' agreed Da, getting into his jacket, 'like everybody else!'

Just then Janey called out that Miss Blackwell's car was in sight and that Mr Blackwell was driving, for the latter had suddenly agreed with his sister that he was behind the times and was doing all he could to rectify that state of affairs.

'How do you know that?' Katy asked. 'You can't see from here who's driving?'

'It's going from side to side,' Janey replied.

On hearing this Da called Janey into the house for it was a well-known fact that Andrew Blackwell, being an impatient man, was slow to learn the driving. Miss Blackwell had given up teaching him after two lessons, protesting that he nearly killed her by running into the hedge with his foot on the accelerator. After that the young man from the town garage took over and progress was better and a little safer.

The car jerked into the doorway, coming to an abrupt stop, and Andrew Blackwell in his working clothes got out.

'I was just getting into my stride,' he said with a broad laugh. 'I wish I had arranged to go with Jessie too.'

'Get into the back, David,' Miss Blackwell called out to Da, as she moved into the driving seat, and Aggie saw she was in her best grey. 'Hughie will sit beside me as he knows the road. Andrew Blackwell's biding at home. There's enough patients in the Infirmary as it is!'

'Oh, Jessie, I'm just anxious to learn the driving,' her brother insisted.

'We'll give your regards to Jamie,' Hughie consoled him as he got out with the starting handle, and Aggie thought that he cut a fine figure in his brown suit.

'Just do that,' returned the farmer, 'and tell him that I'll be along in the motor myself, the next time the bull tosses him!'

The car moved off, with much waving and good wishes, for the doctor's favourable opinion had turned the expedition into a joy-ride, rather than a journey of sympathy.

The house was strange without Da, for like most quiet men he had great authority. His word was law and, although he seldom raised his voice and never his hand—threatening to do so often enough—the family obeyed him without question. All except Ma who had the cleverest way of agreeing with him and asking his opinion, and then doing what she thought best in the long run, with Da believing that it had been his good advice all along.

However, with the Qualifying over and Jamie Watson as well as could be expected, Aggie felt as light as a feather. The day was fresh as only an April day can be, with the dust well laid on the lane, after a cloud had trailed her skirts over the valley.

Ma was in good spirits too on the way to church. 'If God spares us, by next week, I'll have enough saved for John's new suit,' she said to them.

John grinned showing all his fine teeth. 'I'll be glad to be able to move my arms again on Sundays,' he answered.

In the afternoon a quavering voice sounded outside the door and there stood old George Conlon from the town with his hymn book. He was a certain sign of the coming of the brighter days, for he only did the rounds of the farms and cottages on a Sunday afternoon when the good weather was in. As he stood there in his black clothes, his eyes raised piously to the skies and his white beard and hair moving in the little wind, he made a saintly figure, although everybody said he had been a bad rascal in his day. Aggie had heard it said he had married several wives, each unknown to the other, and had dressed up as a minister on another occasion and gone to the bedside of a sick woman. But all that was when he was fresh and in his prime, and Katy had said to Aggie that no doubt he had repented all his sins long ago. As he accepted the penny and the scone and cheese wrapped in paper, he bowed his head humbly and moved on down the lane.

Later Robert and Aggie took a walk over to the river bank. As they crossed the fields now patterned with daisies, Aggie thought of Grandfather Kenny and she wondered how he was faring, for Da had received news that he was bad with rheumatics. She picked a daisy in his name and hoped the good weather would cure him, for he was a man who would take ill with staying in the house all day.

In the Far Orchard the fitful April sunlight dappled with light and shade the twisted branches of the apple trees. From among the growing grass and the mosses, the wild violets poked their little purple heads, and the windflowers fluttered their pale blooms. Along the river bank, now green with the early growth that would bloom in the summer, they met Nathan Thomson with several of his children, red-haired like himself and free as the wind.

Nathan, after enquiring after Jamie Watson, began to tell them all the news and goings-on of the Little Valley, for if Cousin John knew the affairs of the town and country in general, Nathan was acquainted with all the ups and downs of his neighbours.

He related how the gamekeeper had sprained his ankle jumping a ditch thus leaving the fields open to all the poachers in the countryside, that a golden eagle had been seen near Cairnsmore, that the widow in the Gow Farm refused to put her clock the hour forward like everybody else, and that Abie Irvine of the Home Farm was installing one of those new contraptions called a milking-machine in his byre. 'My old mother has milked with her hands all her days, and she's against these unnatural things,' Nathan went on, 'it's bound to upset the animals. The sun and the moon don't suddenly change their times, and there's the tide coming up the river and it doesn't ask anybody if it's too late or too early!'

'Oh, but Nathan,' Robert answered, 'you have to move with the times. It's all machinery nowadays! I'm saving up for a new bike.'

'I suppose a man of my age thinks that things should stay the same as when he was young,' Nathan replied sadly. 'Come out of the reeds, you young scoundrels,' he boomed out to his children, 'or the hand will reach out for you from the water!'

As the children scurried back, Aggie shivered for she imagined she saw the wide ripple of something stirring in the depths.

Before she and Robert turned for home, Nathan asked her to remind Ma that his eldest boy was ashamed to go out, such was his nakedness. Aggie knew he was referring to

John's forthcoming new suit and hinting at what Ma could do with the old one.

When Da arrived home that evening he was received as though he had been gone for years, for it was an event when anybody in the Little Valley travelled so far.

'We had a good day but we're all tired,' Miss Blackwell said from the car. 'Jamie's fine and he was very glad to see us.' Then Hughie Grant pushed a thick stick of pink rock into Aggie's hand 'as a fairin',' and they moved away.

'Jamie's as bright as a lintie!' Da told them all in the house, as everybody, including Cousin John, listened eagerly. 'He has a bandage round his head and one arm in a sling. And that hospital's a tremendous place. And the drive through the countryside was that bonny . . .' and Da went over every detail he could remember until at last nobody could think of anything else to ask.

'You'll be feeling tired, Da?' Ma then asked.

'A bit stiff maybe,' he answered, 'but I could just do the same thing over again tomorrow. A motor-car's a great thing!'

'When I was down at the house this afternoon, Lizzie was writing a letter,' Cousin John remarked, looking at everybody in a secretive fashion.

There was a moment's silence.

'Oh, then!' Ma answered at last. 'We'll just see what happens!'

When Ma said that, Aggie guessed that, like herself and everybody else, she was expecting Auntie Lizzie to take the train and rush to Jamie Watson's bedside in the hospital and forget all about Wallie. But one day followed another with the Easter holidays at hand, and there was still no word of Auntie Lizzie doing any such thing, and as far as Aggie heard she never even mentioned Jamie's name.

The last day of school was always a pleasant one, which made up for the days following the Qualifying. On these days the teacher had made the three candidates do the examination paper over again and after much preaching had announced that she thought they might not have done so badly, but they were not to build up their hopes too high.

'I shall not give any homework during the Easter holidays, for I think everyone should get as much fresh air as possible,' she said, 'but I wish to give special warning to the boys. Do not rob or destroy the birds' nests! If you are collecting eggs, then one from each nest is quite sufficient. As it is, it is a very cruel practice!'

There was a strained silence, for every year at the Easter holidays, many of the town boys spent the time bird-nesting. Aggie had known some sad moments, when, after a troop of them had passed along the lane, she found the little nest torn out of the hedges and the eggs trampled and broken; at the bottom of the hedge a pair of bereaved blackbirds clucked their anguish, and overhead the peewits cried out in warning. Once Aggie had seen a weasel dart out from the dike among a family of young peewits chirping about in the young corn like brown chickens, and it took a handful of stones to scare it off. So she knew that the birds had plenty to reckon with, without the human race turning on them too.

'I'm glad the teacher said that,' Katy announced, as they went out the Big Road, 'eh, Aggie?'

'She was right and I think we'll stop looking into the roadside nests so that there will be no tracks,' Aggie answered.

'Aggie, I heard Da say there was going to be a crow-shooting on Saturday!' Janey called out. This silenced them, for they remembered that last year, when the shoot was on, the crows left their nests in the Castle Wood and flew to the big sauch trees, until the branches were black with them.

'They must have been desperate to forsake their nests,' Da said, 'for the eggs and the young ones would be the prey of all the hawks in the district, with no parent birds to beat them off.'

To Aggie the crows were cackling gossips, the way they could sit on trees watching the folk and changing places all the time on the branches to pass funny remarks, but the countryside would not be the same without them. They were as much part of it as the trees.

'What will we do in the holidays, Aggie?' Katy then asked.

'There's plenty to do,' replied Aggie. 'For one thing Ma says she'll visit Mrs McClurg, then we can get out the "birlies", and we have that bit of stable rope for skips, and Jamie Watson will be home next week and Miss Blackwell says she'll take us for a run in the motor!' And then she added, 'and I have two new library books in my bag that the teacher gave me.'

'Oh, isn't that a lot!' exclaimed Janey.

'Don't forget about the new Catalogue!' Katy reminded them. 'We have to pick our summer frocks and all out of it yet!'

'I'm picking straw hats and white shoes as well!' said Janey grandly.

'You can pick anything you like,' Katy answered to that. 'We got new summer frocks last year and Ma says they'll do this year again. Oh, but I wish we had shoes for all that!'

'When I was at the Qualifying, nobody had button boots but me,' said Aggie. 'I don't care what I've got on out here on the road, but I just hate when the town ones are looking!'

'Oh well, they won't be looking at us for nearly two weeks,' Katy said brightly, as she started to whirl herself round in the lane, 'nor the teacher either! And this is Easter Sunday this week-end. We'll have boiled eggs for the breakfast instead of fried ones!'

During the Easter holidays the spring, so slow to start, advanced with giant strides and the brown and grey of the hillsides turned to green. Ma crossed the fields to visit the McClurgs in the Hill Village with the girls and as Aggie looked down from the brae-top at the patchwork quilt of the Little Valley, she saw the colours had changed there too.

'It's the best time of the year,' Roddie greeted them, 'especially if you have something young to work for.'

'Now then, Roderick,' said his wife sharply, 'don't question the will of God. Come on inside, Mrs Kenny. I'm fair pleased to see you!'

'I suppose you're right,' answered her husband, looking along the rough stony hill-top road, to where the two old McBurnie sisters were seated outside their cottage smoking clay pipes. 'There's these two women. They've lost count of their age, but they're well in the nineties. They've never been farther than the town and never been on a train. There's no accounting for some things!' and he shook his head in bewilderment.

As they bent their heads to enter the doorway, low under the thatched roof, Aggie wondered if Mrs McClurg would bring another gingerbread out of the box like last time.

On the next Sunday afternoon, Miss Blackwell drove down to the house in the motor and Ma and the three girls got in.

'We'll take a run down the bay,' she said. 'Maybe you would all like to see the sea!'

Aggie felt just like one of the rich Miss Robbs, sitting in the back seat next to Katy and Janey with the plaid over their knees, the only difference being that the Miss Robbs' motor was very big and it took two men to manage it, one to drive and the other to get out and open the door.

'I'd rather have Miss Blackwell,' whispered Katy, with her uncanny way of knowing Aggie's thoughts.

Aggie nodded. Miss Blackwell was in great spirits these days and there was never a mention of her bad leg keeping her in at all.

At Nathan Thomson's cottage Ma got out with John's outgrown suit, for she had bought him a new navy serge during the week, which was perhaps a little bit big, but would last all the longer. It would not have been the right thing to send Aggie in with the parcel, as Nathan was an old acquaintance and Ma felt she had to spend a minute asking after the family. Nearly every time Aggie saw Mrs Thomson she had a new baby, wrapped in the shawl she wore round her shoulders, and even now red-haired children of all ages, from toddlers to early teens, were standing staring solemnly at the motor-car and those inside it.

When Ma came out, they set off again, passed 'God-is-Love' cottage where the preacher lived and turned on to the Big Road.

Katy and Janey chattered to each other but Aggie stared silently out of the window, for there was a lot to look at. Primroses and early bluebells and white clumps of stars of Bethlehem grew on the banks and shady places by the side of the road, and the young lambs leaped and frolicked and pretended to be frightened by the new-fangled vehicle on the highway. For a short time the railway-line kept company with the road and then took off into the hills and all the mystery that lay beyond; the road began to climb and then looked down at the river now flowing into the bay.

Aggie tingled with excitement for here was the world, with motor-cars round every bend, folk on bicycles, a man on a tricycle, and a horse-drawn brake just ahead, filled with people, stiff in their Sunday clothes. As Miss Blackwell passed the brake, Aggie wondered if the horse had any hard feelings when all these new inventions were leaving him behind. It came into her mind that Da had once said an animal was both humble and proud, and folk were often just ignorant. She felt it would be ignorant to turn round and look at the horse, so she kept her eyes fixed on the grey-green waters of the bay that lay at the foot of the slopes.

Then Miss Blackwell turned the car round as both she and Ma had to be back for the milking.

'We'll come back in the warm weather,' she told them, 'and go down to the shore for a paddle. The Lord will not mind us enjoying the Sabbath, I'm sure of that, for we have just no time through the week to enjoy anything!'

She took the long way back to the house, by the Big Road, meeting many of the townspeople out for their Sunday walk, among them being Cathie Gemmell with her mother and father. Katy and Janey waved with great energy.

'I hope she saw us!' Katy said to Aggie. 'She's got on a new brown coat and hat but we are in a motor-car.'

Aggie only nodded. They would know soon enough for the school started on Tuesday.

Although all their lives the folk of the Little Valley were used to hearing talk of weather and crops, and late and early harvests, yet the changing from one season to another was always as fresh each year as it had been the one before. When Nathan Thomson said the swallows were back, everybody was interested and the first call of the cuckoo was listened for keenly; an announcement was printed in the paper if one of the quality thought they had been the first to hear it.

The cuckoo ushered in the summer. When Aggie heard it May was on the doorstep and the trees in the Little Wood were nearly all in leaf, except the ash which was always late, and the big oak tree that had been struck by lightning. There it stood, gaunt and bare the whole year round and never again would it feel the wind swirling through pale green skirts in the early summer, for it would forever be an outcast.

'Look, Aggie,' Katy exclaimed on the way home from school, 'there's a buttercup! Let's see if you like butter!' and she picked it and held it under her sister's chin.

'Everybody likes butter,' said Janey from behind. 'It shines below everybody's chin!'

'No, that's not true,' argued Katy, 'for last night in the byre Miss Blackwell said to Ma—oh, Aggie,' she broke off suddenly, 'do you know what else they said in the byre?'

'No.' Aggie shifted the coats she was carrying from one arm to the other.

'That Auntie Lizzie had been to see Jamie Watson since he came home and Alice Robinson went with her!'

'What for would Alice go too, Aggie?' Janey asked.

'Women are not supposed to visit men by themselves,' Aggie explained patiently. 'It's bad manners.' Then she turned to Katy. 'Maybe Auntie Lizzie and Jamie are back on,' she said hopefully.

'I couldn't make any more out,' answered Katy, 'but we'll see the next time she comes out. Maybe Jamie will get christened because he got a fright from the bull!'

On Auntie Lizzie's next visit, Aggie listened hard for any mention of Jamie Watson, but the evening wore on and the time for her departure came nearer and still there was neither wheesht nor whisper about him. Any minute too Wallie Johnstone's knock would be heard on the door and Auntie Lizzie would get ready to be escorted home.

'Wallie's late tonight,' Ma said, looking up at the clock.

'He's not coming tonight,' replied Auntie Lizzie getting into her coat, 'nor any other night.'

Aggie could hardly believe her ears, and she saw that the rest of the family were equally surprised.

'Lizzie, do you know what you're doing?' Ma said at last and there was a deep frown on her face.

'Yes, I do,' replied Auntie Lizzie, in a very husky voice. 'Jamie's not fit to come this far and it's not fair to encourage Wallie any longer. I'll never marry Wallie anyway, so I told him I'd see myself home. The nights are clear enough now too.'

Aggie gulped and a lump rose in her throat, for she had never heard talk like this in her life before.

'Oh, but Lizzie, the boys will see you along the road a bit, for it will be dark before you reach the town,' Da assured her.

'And what did Wallie say to all this?' Ma wanted to know.

'He's hoping I'll change my mind,' replied Auntie Lizzie and there was a quiver in her voice. 'He says he'll wait a while yet. He's a very decent man, Wallie.'

As she set off up the lane with Robert and John, Aggie realized that the worst had happened. Auntie Lizzie had nobody, just nobody. This thought made her feel so sad and heavy that, after Katy and Janey were in bed, and she was washing herself in the pantry, she took her time about soaping the flannel and rubbing it over her face.

Ma and Da, alone in the kitchen, were speaking in low

tones to each other for such things as courtships were never discussed in front of children. Aggie paid little attention until she could not help hearing that Ma's tones were a little excited.

'That's what it is,' she heard Ma say, 'she made Jamie jealous, and now that there's less reason to be jealous, she's giving him a chance to consider a few things. I wouldn't be surprised . . .' but Aggie heard no more for Ma's voice dropped back into a whisper.

When Aggie got into bed, she lay and wondered how long Jamie would take to make up his mind this time, for he was a man who never did anything in a hurry.

Chapter Thirteen

THE Little Valley was filled with the scent of blossom for it was near the end of May and summer had come. Here and there in the hedges, now frothy white with maythorn, showed the pink blush of the first wild roses, and along by the river, where the reeds were now as tall as a man, the sloe bushes were a mass of creamy flowers. On the hillsides the colours were the brightest for the yellow of the whins and the broom that glowed there was shown off by the bluebells among the sprouting bracken. Even on the wet days a pale golden light lay on the fields, and when the wind passed over the long grass of the hay crop, it was a caress of light and shade.

To Aggie the coming of the summer was like the keeping of a promise. The dark days of winter, now almost unbelievable, and the cold and moody days of spring, were things you had to bear, and in return you got the summer—the summer when long warm days stretched before you without end.

'Eternity,' Mrs McMinn had tried to explain to the school, 'is without end.' They had all nodded wisely in complete agreement but without understanding. Yet now when Aggie saw a great procession of white-topped clouds with dark undersides, marching from beyond the town across the sky, teasing Cairnsmore with their blue shadows, and darkening the Little Valley for a passing moment, she wondered if the sight had something to do with eternity.

She did not wonder for long, for early summer is no time for deep thought when you are just coming twelve—especially as Mrs McMinn had already found a new outlet for the energies of her pupils.

'The religious examination takes place in the second week in June. That leaves a very short time for preparation!' was her daily cry. Even the Inspector was forgotten and the Qualifying was hardly mentioned. So most of the school day was spent in reciting the ten commandments and learning the parables, with the older ones helping to teach the younger ones.

Every day Mrs McMinn took a few minutes to hear Katy's scales and teach her the new song 'Gently, gently sighs the breeze.' Sometimes Cathie Gemmell played the notes on the piano and Mrs McMinn watched that Katy opened her mouth wide enough and was soft or loud at the right places. She was very strict about 'control of the voice' and slurring of words, and while this was going on the rest of the school were supposed to be deep in catechism, although everybody was listening.

It was early in the afternoon on the last Wednesday in May when Mrs McMinn, who had started the afternoon with a geography lesson and was thundering at Tom Riley for not being better acquainted with the railways of Britain, that footsteps were heard crossing the playground and entering the school porch. The outer door creaked open, men's voices murmured, and two large shadows appeared on the frosted glass of the schoolroom door.

'It's the inspector,' Eddie Campbell hissed to the listening school, whereupon Mrs McMinn whipped the cane off her desk, pushed it to the back of the window-still, and was ready to open the door in answer to the knocking, with only a pencil in her hand and a gracious smile on her face.

It was the inspector, along with another gentleman, as tall and thin and glum-looking as the inspector was round and beaming and rosy.

Aggie's heart turned a somersault as she stood up with the rest and said 'Good-afternoon, sirs,' as Mrs McMinn had taught them. 'It has nothing to do with the Qualifying! He comes every year anyway!' she told herself, as she got out a reading book, for the teacher had trained them what to do when the Inspector came. 'Continue with whatever work you're doing,' she had drilled them again and again, 'unless it is a blackboard exercise. In that case take out a reading or a history or geography book, whichever one is your best subject!'

The inspector, after shaking hands with the teacher, introduced the tall man as Dr Crawford, laid his hat and brief-case on the teacher's desk and then smiled jovially at everybody. After that he asked to see the Register while Dr Crawford went round the walls, peering at the drawings, most of them Cathie Gemmell's, and the maps, with what— to Aggie—seemed a very sour look. She did notice, however, that he looked twice at the drawing of Janey's pig looking over the edge of the sty, but everybody did that because the pig's expression was so knowing that you just could not help yourself.

Then Aggie heard the inspector mention the Qualifying Class and Mrs McMinn rattled out the three names and asked them to stand up. Aggie shuffled to her feet, tried to look pleasant, and wished with all her heart that she was running in the green grass near home, even if she had just put her bare foot on a thistle.

'Which one is Agnes Kenny?' asked the inspector.

'This is Agnes,' replied Mrs McMinn briskly, 'a very good pupil and a most conscientious worker too!' and Aggie thought she detected a glassy threat in the teacher's eye if she did not try hard enough to live up to this good character.

'Tell me, Agnes,' said the inspector pleasantly, 'how old are you?'

'Twelve in July, sir.'

'Just so. Mm!' he paused. 'I would like to ask you a few questions, Agnes. Nothing very difficult, of course. A short test of general knowledge, so to speak.'

'Yes, sir.' Aggie whispered the words and felt just like a rabbit in one of Wallie Johnstone's traps. She clasped her hands tight behind her to still their trembling and waited.

'Now then, Agnes,' he began . . .

And so the inspector went through the coal fields of Britain, a small part of the history of Scotland, a mention of Sir Walter Scott and Dickens, and Aggie's confidence grew, while Mrs McMinn, standing a few paces behind the inspector, registered approval with a slow nod of her head up and down, or a little warning shake from one side to the other. And all the time she kept her eyes meekly lowered to the floor.

Dr Crawford seemed to be entirely occupied with his own thoughts and kept his eyes fixed on the smoky ceiling, as though it was the only point of the room worth his interest.

Then the inspector's questions went further into the world.

'Who were the Pilgrim Fathers?'

'Who was Captain Cook?'

Aggie remembered him just in time and after Cathie Gemmell had put up her hand and snapped her fingers to answer it.

The last one was about the shortest sea route to Australia. The shortest sea route to Australia? For the life of her, Aggie could not think of it. She tried to picture the map of the world with Australia, coloured pink, lying at the bottom right hand corner. Australia, where Ritchie lived!

A nervous sweat was beginning to break out on her forehead for there was Cathie Gemmell and Helen McKay both snapping their fingers with the answer. She tried to see something on Mrs McMinn's face but her eyes were down-cast and her mouth a thin line. She was aware too of Katy looking at her with anxious eyes, but still the answer would not come.

'Sit down, Agnes,' said the inspector at last. 'Does anybody else know the answer?'

'Through the Suez Canal!' Cathie Gemmell said it first and Aggie felt terribly ashamed. She just could not under-stand how it could have slipped her mind. 'Everybody knows about the Suez Canal,' she told herself in a sort of panic. 'I suppose that's me out of the Qualifying! Maybe the inspector was giving me a last chance to help me out with my paper. The teacher said he might do that!' She smiled briefly at Katy to try to hide the misery she felt, but her sister had no answering smile. When Katy was unhappy she never tried to hide it, and her small face looked ready for tears.

After that the inspector asked Cathie Gemmell and Helen MaKay a few questions and their answers came as smartly as hailstones falling on a tin roof, although Aggie thought the questions were not quite as difficult as the ones she had been asked.

'I expect that they have passed all right, and he doesn't have to bother with them!' was the only consolation she could find and this increased her gloom.

When he had gone round most of the school, not taking any more notice of Aggie, he turned and smiled to Mrs McMinn. 'The standard of work is very high indeed, Mrs McMinn,' he smiled to the teacher. 'Let me congratulate you!'

Mrs McMinn blushed and answered, 'Thank you, Inspector. We all do our best!'

Aggie sighed inwardly. 'All except me!' she thought. 'Oh, why didn't I think of the Suez Canal? What will I say to Ma? She'll be awfully disappointed!'

'There's just one thing more,' the inspector said, looking round the school. 'My friend here,' he bowed slightly to Dr Crawford who just scowled at them, 'is very fond of music. Is there anybody here can sing or play?'

There was a moment's pause, but only a moment. Before the teacher had a chance to suggest somebody, Aggie saw Katy's little figure shoot up from her desk.

'Please sir,' she said in a trembling voice, 'I can sing.'

'Oh, indeed.' Dr Crawford spoke for the first time and he looked at Katy with a new interest. 'What can you sing?'

'Oh, Rowan Tree!'

'A lovely old song too! Just let me hear it!'

Katy squeezed past Dora Jones, who sat at the end of the desk, and stood up in the passage between the rows. Clasping her hands behind her back she raised her head.

'Oh, Rowan Tree, Oh, Rowan Tree,' she began with just a faint shakiness in her voice.

'Thou'lt aye be dear tae me.'

Already the nervousness had gone and Katy's sweet tones were ringing through the schoolroom. As she continued Aggie fixed her eyes on the doctor's face with awe, for it was as though he had taken off a mask. As he stood there listening to Katy, his face wore such an expression of pleasure that he did not seem the same man who had been staring up at the ceiling a few moments before.

When Katy reached the top note, a little smile wavered at the corner of the doctor's mouth, and Aggie saw the heads of the passers-by collecting outside the school wall in the sunlight.

Katy was singing her best. She was being careful over her words and the soft and loud notes as Mrs McMinn had been teaching her for so long, and Aggie knew she was trying to make up for her own failure to answer the inspector's last question, by singing as well as she could. Standing there with her thin little neck and head raised, Aggie could not help comparing her sister to a yearling thrush, for they had the same slender look and young fluting voice.

When the last notes died away there was a little burst of clapping outside the school wall, but a deep stillness reigned in the schoolroom.

'Well!' Dr Crawford broke the silence and went forward

185

slowly to Katy, looking down at her from his great height. 'I never expected this. What is your name, little girl?'

'Katy—Katherine Kenny, sir. That's my sister Agnes, over there!' she answered breathlessly.

'Katy Kenny,' repeated the doctor thoughtfully and he sat down on the edge of her desk. 'How old are you, Katy?'

'Eleven in June, sir.'

'And who taught you to sing like that?'

'The teacher, sir.'

'Indeed!' Dr Crawford flashed a small smile at Mrs Mc-Minn. 'Can you sing anything else?'

'Yes, sir. "Gently, gently sighs the breeze".'

'Can you sing if I play the piano?' Dr Crawford then asked.

'Yes, sir.'

'Come over to the piano with me then, Katy. I should like to hear you sing again!'

The whole school, now intensely interested, watched Katy walk carefully over to the piano, and Aggie saw that one long boot-lace was flapping loose.

When Dr Crawford's hands rippled over the keys a quiet fell once more in the schoolroom and along the wall outside, and at a nod from him Katy began her second song. She sang it as carefully and sweetly as the first one and Aggie thought how pleased Ma and Da would be when they knew about this, and what a pity they had never heard Katy sing with the doctor playing the piano. The song ended and the clapping outside was loud and long.

The doctor turned his head. 'Now, listen carefully to me, Katy!' he said slowly. 'You have been blessed with this great gift of a beautiful singing voice. There are not many people so gifted. I am a doctor of music and I know something about it!'

'Yes, sir!' Katy almost whispered it.

'Now, listen carefully again! Mrs McMinn, your teacher, has done a splendid job of the early training of your voice. You are very fortunate in having such a teacher!'

186

At this the teacher bowed her head in acknowledgment, and Aggie saw her face was pink with pleasure.

'I sincerely hope,' the doctor went on, 'that Mrs McMinn will continue and I ask you to do everything that she tells you in this matter!'

'Yes, sir!'

'I shall come back during the next school year to hear you again and I shall make a point of following your progress with the greatest interest.'

'That's very kind of you, Dr Crawford!' Mrs McMinn fairly crowed and Aggie swallowed. 'I shall certainly do all I can to help Katherine.'

'Thank you, Mrs McMinn. I can depend on you,' he replied graciously and turned again to Katy. 'I hope, Katy that you pay great attention to your schoolwork so that you can sit the Qualifying examination like your sister Agnes over there!'

He smiled briefly towards Agnes, who grew red at being caught staring, although everybody else was doing the same. 'You must have an education to go with your talents. You may go back to your seat, Katy, and thank you for a lovely performance!'

Katy trudged over to her desk, smiled slightly at Janey on her way past and threw a quick glance towards Aggie as she slid into her seat. Aggie saw her eyes were bright and shining.

'I never expected to find a little songbird, when I decided to come with the inspector, Mrs McMinn,' the doctor boomed happily to the teacher. 'Life can hold such wonderful surprises!'

'So it can,' agreed the inspector, who had kept in the background during the musical interlude. 'I also have some surprises which I don't think I ought to keep to myself any longer either,' and he unclasped his brief-case and drew out a long envelope. Hardly daring to breathe, Aggie watched the inspector take a paper from the envelope and carefully unfold it. She saw that Mrs McMinn had clasped her hands tightly in front of her, and her eyes were glued fearfully to the paper in his hand.

'It has to do with those who sat the Qualifying Examination,' the inspector continued quietly, 'and I shall not keep them in suspense any longer. Of the three who sat, all passed.'

'Oh!'

Aggie could not restrain the terrible gasp of relief as she realized what the inspector had said. She had passed the Qualifying! They had all passed! She turned towards Katy as she felt the tears rise in her eyes. Ma and Da wouldn't be disappointed after all. Wouldn't they be pleased! And the boys as well! And she thought she had failed!

'Indeed, Inspector,' she heard the teacher say. 'That is most gratifying!'

'There is something more,' the inspector went on in the same quiet voice. 'One pupil, Agnes Kenny, although one of the youngest candidates, had the highest marks in the county. Her English paper was especially good. She had very high marks for her essay!'

'Oh!'

This time the school gasped and somewhere in the distance, Aggie heard Eddie Campbell rumble, 'Good Old Aggie!'

Maybe it was the excitement or the heat or just that she was hungry, but the room darkened suddenly and the teacher's desk and the blackboard began to swing from one side to the other. 'Ma will say it's because I'm growing!' she said to herself and clutched her desk hard until her vision cleared.

'A good pupil,' she heard Mrs McMinn say a long way off, 'a conscientious worker!'

But the inspector was speaking to her again and everything was settling back into its place.

'I asked you these questions, Agnes, just to make sure,' he beamed at her. 'You answered them all correctly but one. That was a very good achievement. We are all very proud of you, Agnes!'

Aggie gulped and then reddened and tried to say, 'Thank you, sir,' and smile instead of weep, for the inspector's announcement was just beginning to have its full effect. The highest marks in the county! It would take her a long time to believe that it was she, Agnes Kenny, who had managed that!

'Oh, this has been a great afternoon for us all!' Mrs McMinn fluttered and Aggie had never seen her so excited.

'There's not much of the afternoon left, I'm afraid,' the inspector said, taking out his watch from his waistcoat pocket. 'It's almost half-past three! I think, Mrs McMinn, everybody will want to get home with the news, and I have said all I came to say,' and he looked round the pupils as though he would be grateful for their opinion.

'Yes, sir,' the whole school echoed just as though everybody had passed the Qualifying.

'Then, Dr Crawford, it's time we went too,' and he picked up his hat and his brief-case.

Once more the school rose up and said 'Good afternoon, sirs,' and this time the tone was loud and sincere. Both gentlemen shook hands once again with Mrs McMinn, the inspector turned to beam at them all, Dr Crawford waggled a long teasing finger in Katy's direction, smiled bleakly at the rest of them, and gradually they drifted through the schoolroom door with the teacher attending them to the porch.

The school was too well disciplined to make much noise when the teacher was out, but everybody could whisper and everybody did and the room was full of hisses.

'Aggie,' Eddie Campbell wanted to know, 'can I go out to help you tell your Ma?'

'There's three of us to tell her,' Katy retorted.

'Eddie, you can go and tell Grandma and Granda Breen if you like,' Aggie suggested because she never liked to hurt anybody.

'I'll go with him,' Tom Riley whispered loudly.

'Me, too,' said Bernard Jones.

Aggie nodded. She had never known such joyous excitement all her days and the whole school shared it. They all agreed that Katy had never sung so well, and they were all pleased that one of their school had beaten all the others in marks.

And all three had passed the Qualifying. That was the main thing.

Aggie heard Janey's voice calling her and she caught sight of her little sister trying to tell her something, but just then a small piece of rubber stung her cheek and she looked round to hear Bernard Jones tell her that the school would not be the same after she had left it.

'Here's the teacher!' Eddie Campbell, who missed nothing, warned everybody.

The noise ceased abruptly as Mrs McMinn's quick footsteps were heard approaching the schoolroom. The teacher was smiling happily for it had been a day of victory for her too, but as she stood at her desk Aggie saw that she had the same tired look she had seen on Ma's face at the end of a long day.

'Attention, everyone!' she called out sharply, and after a moment, resumed in an even voice, 'You all heard what the inspector said. I shall go over it again very briefly. The standard of work is very good indeed, and everyone answered the questions in a most satisfactory manner. All three candidates of the Qualifying class passed the examination. That means they will be leaving our little school after this term to continue their education in a much bigger and more advanced one. All three worked for their success and Agnes Kenny was given the special grace to bring the highest honour to herself and to our school. Let us be deeply grateful to Almighty God for this grace and may it be forever in you all, whatever you set out to do. Now, all kneel and pray!'

All through prayers Aggie could not help thinking of Mr McMinn's unhappy face and she wished she could have replaced it with a brighter one for the teacher's sake. She wished too she could say some words of thanks to the teacher but the blanket of shyness that always suffocated her would never permit such words to be heard.

She joined the others in the chorus of 'Good afternoon, ma'am' and went to get her coat off the peg. Half-heartedly she slung her bag over her shoulder, before picking up her coat, letting the others go on through the porch, for only the country ones had coats with them.

Something urged her to turn back. Hanging the coat up again she mumbled to Katy that she had forgotten something and returned to the schoolroom. The teacher was tidying up her desk when she came in.

'Well, Agnes?' she asked.

'Please, ma'am,' Aggie breathed hard and said the only thing she could think of. 'My mother and father will be very pleased.'

For a moment Mrs McMinn gravely studied her pupil's face and then she smiled brightly.

'How nice of you to say that, Agnes!' she said. 'I know your parents will be pleased, although I must admit you worked well too. You may tell your mother I shall walk out some Sunday afternoon and have a little talk with her. There are a few things I should like to discuss.'

'Yes, ma'am,' Aggie smiled back and thought how nice the teacher was when she wasn't teaching.

'And I must say I have never heard Katherine sing so well!' she beamed.

'Yes, ma'am.' Aggie's smile widened for she liked to hear her sisters praised, beyond anything.

'A very successful afternoon.' The teacher picked up the register and the exercise books which she was intending to take home with her. 'You have a great deal to tell your parents.'

'Yes, ma'am. Good afternoon, ma'am,' replied Aggie and she left the schoolroom with the feeling that the teacher knew what she had tried to say. She joined Katy and Janey, who were swinging on the school-gate, and they went down the hill alone for the rest of the school had gone their own ways.

At the foot of the hill the shop-keeper, who gave a big bag of broken biscuits for a penny, was standing at his shop-door.

'So you passed the Qualifying, Agnes,' he smiled to her. 'That's the stuff!'

Aggie was surprised at his knowing.

'The boys told me,' he explained.

Crossing the bridge two ladies of the town stopped them.

'I hear, Agnes, that you did extra well in your examination,' one said. 'I could not help overhearing the Campbell boy telling someone else.'

Aggie blushed. 'Yes, ma'am. The inspector told us today,' she answered and then she remembered seeing them in Miss Blackwell's parlour away back on Hallowe'en.

'That's splendid,' the other lady said. 'Your parents will get a fine surprise when they hear this. Our regards to Miss Blackwell when you see her.'

'Aggie, you're famous,' Katy said as soon as they had got clear of the town, for they were bursting to talk and were only waiting for the long bare road that lay before them to begin.

'You're the one that's going to be famous,' Aggie replied. 'That Dr Crawford said he would follow your progress. I can hardly believe all the things that happened this afternoon. I nearly felt queer!'

'Fancy having a doctor for music! That's queer enough!' Janey said and Aggie noticed, to her great surprise, that her little sister was trotting in front of them instead of at the back as was her usual way.

'Aggie.' It was Janey again. 'Will you let me tell Ma about the Qualifying?'

'Oh, no,' Katy retorted, 'you'll be telling Ma about me when I pass the Qualifying. That would be twice.'

'You can tell Ma about Katy singing,' Aggie suggested, and then she remembered Janey trying to tell her something in the schoolroom when the teacher was out. 'What did you want to say when Bernard Jones hit me with the rubber?'

Janey's lip trembled a little. 'I wondered if you saw that the doctor looked at my pig twice.'

'I saw that,' Katy answered generously.

'So did I,' Aggie agreed. 'He must have liked it,' and she saw Janey's face clear up. 'Ma will be pleased about that, too!' and she took her little sister's hand.

When they left the Big Road and turned into the dusty lane there was no mention of anybody taking off the heavy boots to pad through the dust in bare feet, for there was no time to spare. The lushness of summer lay on the roadsides, now deep in grass with buttercups, lady-blue-eyes, and the first campions growing alongside the wild parsley and kernels, and the pink and white creepers that twined through the hedge. The air was scented with clover and blossom and grasses and all the wild fragrance that makes up the smell of summer.

The first thing the girls saw when they entered the lane were two people a long way ahead.

'There's two folk!' Katy cried. 'A man and a woman!'

'I hope it's not visitors!' Aggie sighed, 'because we'll never get a chance to talk!'

However, the couple in front were not in any hurry and the girls were. As the distance shortened between them, they saw to their surprise that it was Auntie Lizzie and Jamie Watson.

'It can't be!' said Aggie, shading her eyes from the sunlight.

'But it is!' insisted Katy, 'and she has her arm through his, and it's broad daylight!'

'Everything's happening today!' Janey voiced her opinion in some bewilderment, as she turned round to the other two.

'I wish you'd keep your place at the back, like you did before,' was Katy's irritable answer.

Janey paid no need but merely kept up her trotting ahead of them.

'That means that Jamie and Auntie Lizzie are back on!' said Aggie. 'I'm glad, for I didn't like to see her by herself.'

'That'll be Wallie Johnstone back at the poaching,' was Katy's answer, 'unless he drowns himself!'

'Drowns himself!' echoed Janey in a horrified voice.

'Mm. That's what they do when nobody loves them. I saw it in the paper,' Katy replied smugly.

'If Wallie Johnstone ever jumps into the water, it will be after a salmon,' said Aggie surprised at her own smartness, and they all took a sudden fit of laughter.

'Oh, Aggie, wasn't it terrible when you couldn't answer the last question to the inspector,' Katy spluttered, 'and I didn't know the answer myself! I thought it would help if I sang well!'

'It cheered me up to hear some of us doing something well, for I thought, because I couldn't answer one question that I had failed in everything,' Aggie replied. 'And you did sing well, just like the teacher told you!'

'I tried to. I tried my hardest,' and Aggie watched Katy set her little chin in a stubborn line. 'And I'll do the same the next time the doctor comes back.'

By the time they passed the Little Wood, Auntie Lizzie and Jamie were round the bend but they had almost caught up with them at the Farm. The couple showed no signs of waiting for them either, but just turned to wave a greeting now and then, and walk on.

As Miss Blackwell happened to be lifting some washing which was bleaching on the orchard grass, they had to stop to deliver her friends' message.

'They sent their regards,' Aggie said and added shyly, 'I passed the Qualifying!'

'Oh Agnes, that's grand!' and Miss Blackwell came over to the hedge to speak to them. 'That's great news! And your mother and father will be fair delighted!'

All three kept silent about the high marks, for each one wanted Ma to be the first to be told.

By the time they left the farm, Auntie Lizzie and Jamie were almost at the cottage.

'Let's run!' Katy said and she set off at a trot down the dusty lane with Janey panting behind her. It was too warm for Aggie to run for besides her own coat and schoolbag, she had Janey's as well, and she always liked to go slow in the Hollow to see if any more roses had come out during the day.

Just then the pig heard their voices and began to squeal.

'Henry!' she called out, 'Henry!' and the squeals became grunts, for he was the kind of pig whose excitement subsided as soon as he was noticed.

When she arrived at the cottage, she found Auntie Lizzie and Jamie Watson telling something to Ma, with Katy and Janey looking at them all with the greatest interest.

'As I was saying,' Jamie was relating to Ma in his quiet way, 'when a man has been brought up to believe something, it is very hard for that man to change his opinions. And forbye, he maybe feels disloyal to them that went before him!'

'Aye, Jamie,' Ma replied. 'That I understand well enough.'

'But I've had time to think this while back, and I believe that when a man's on his own he can please himself.'

There was a moment's silence.

'I got christened this morning in the church and then I went to speak to Lizzie's father and mother,' he added humbly. He paused and looked at Auntie Lizzie, who began to blush.

'We're getting married in June, in about four weeks' time,' she said to Ma and her voice trembled slightly. 'We've waited long enough!' and she took Jamie's arm.

'Oh, isn't that nice, sister!' Ma replied in a high kind of voice and Aggie was sure she was crying a little. 'That's the best news I've heard for a long time. I know you'll get on very well together. You'll not get a better man than Jamie!'

'Oh here!' laughed Jamie with a shake of his head.

'And it won't be a quiet wedding either,' Auntie Lizzie then smiled. 'My father wants all the family to be there, since I'll be the last to get married! He says it's time we had some rejoicing!'

'Maybe Katy will sing for us!' Jamie said.

'Katy has been singing today already!' Janey called out. 'She sang for the doctor and he says he'll come back next year again!'

'What doctor?' Ma wanted to know.

'The music doctor. He came with the inspector.'

'Oh, was the inspector there today!' Ma's interest in education flared back up again. 'What did he have to say?'

'He said,' Katy uttered the words slowly, savouring their importance, 'that Aggie had brought great honour to the school. She had the highest marks in the Qualifying!'

'What's that?' Ma reached for a chair as all three told her at once while it was the turn of Auntie Lizzie and Jamie to stand listening in astonishment.

'Katy sang "Oh, Rowan Tree!". He said she had a beautiful singing voice.'

'Cathie Gemmell and Helen McKay passed too but our Aggie had the highest marks in the county!'

'He looked at my pig twice, the doctor did!'

'Is that stewed rhubarb? The teacher says she'll be out to see you some day.'

'A wedding! Oh Ma, will there be dancing?'

'And Aggie thought she hadn't passed because she forgot about the Suez Canal.'

'Fancy, Jamie's christened at last! I hope you didn't get too wet, Jamie!'

'Now we know what to say when folk ask!'

At last Ma got everything sorted out and she sat there, with the sun streaming into the kitchen and now and then wiping her eyes with the corner of her apron.

'Your Da and the boys are clearing out a ditch beyond the hayfield,' she said at last to Aggie. 'You could go and tell them. I'll make Lizzie and Jamie a cup of tea in a minute! I made some fresh oatcakes today!'

'Don't bother about tea for us,' Auntie Lizzie answered, 'I'll see to that,' for she knew her way about the house.

'Oh well then,' Ma said, 'I'll just take a scoop of Indian corn out to the hens, before I get ready for the byre.'

'I'll go and tell Da!' Aggie announced eagerly, skipping to the door, 'and about the wedding too, eh, Auntie Lizzie?'

'Don't stay long for you haven't had anything to eat yet!' Ma called out, 'and you're growing fast!'

Aggie crossed the lane to the field gate. Mounting it, she swung one leg over the top bar and looked round her. At that moment a raucous bird voice rang out from a far corner of the hayfield. 'That's a corncrake!' she cried out. With her leg still perched on the top of the gate, she stayed still and listened, and then she turned her head to look back at the house. Katy and Janey were both standing at the door staring after her, their faces screwed up against the sun, and Ma was on her way to the hen house with her apron full of Indian corn.

There was something forlorn about her sisters standing there watching her going away from them and she hesitated uneasily and wondered.

When Robert was old enough to go on his rambles, he had taken John along with him and as Aggie grew older she was taken too, for that was the pattern of a family. Now with her brothers growing up it was her turn to continue the pattern and there were Katy and Janey waiting.

'I believe I feel different,' she was thinking to herself. 'Maybe when things happen to you, you grow older. A lot happened today.'

It flashed through her mind that the greatest surprise— and relief—had been Jamie Watson's christening. That had been something nobody ever expected to happen, and even yet it was hard to believe that Auntie Lizzie would get settled at last.

The hoarse bird-voice called again and all other thoughts fled as she laughed over to her sisters. 'We can look for the corncrake's nest after we've been to Da and the boys!' she called out to them. 'Come on. I'm waiting for you!'

The little girls scampered across the road and joined Aggie on the gate, then they all dropped down into the long grass.

Ma went on to the hens. They had no need of Indian corn, but she had to get away to think and the hens were her friends. There was a lot to think about what with Lizzie's wedding so soon, and Agnes going to the High School after the summer, and the music doctor's praise of Katy's voice. She could not count her blessings this day for they were so many, but she was thankful for them all, and especially grateful to Mrs McMinn. That was a fine teacher. She had encouraged Agnes, and trained Katy to sing the right way, and advised John to go to the night-school for his future betterment. There were not many like her for she brought the best out in all her pupils.

Throwing the corn to the clucking hens Ma did some calculating. The girls' last year's best summer frocks, with the big let-down, and the straw hats with the daisy trimming, would do for the wedding, because everybody looked at the bride anyway. But maybe she could manage a pair each of those brown one-strap shoes that they were always looking at in the shoe-shop window. Button boots were out of fashion now anyway. Hardly anybody wore them. With the boys both working and Agnes earning a little in the summer holidays things were not just so bad. And if the pig kept thriving . . . She hardly dared plan too much on the pig for fear something might go wrong again.

When she thought of Agnes' success a thrill of pride raced through her. That was the greatest surprise of all. Indeed she had hoped and prayed that Agnes would manage to pass for her own sake and would have been humbly grateful for that. Highest marks in the county! What would Da think of that?

She fixed her eye on a plump brown hen. 'You'll go to Mrs McMinn!' she said firmly.

A smile passed over her face as she heard her girls' young voices over in the fields. The young ones were all right with Agnes, just as Agnes had been safe with her brothers.

Standing for a moment she looked round her. The Little Valley was a bonny place when there was time to look at it, with the Barrhill and Larg, fresh and green with early summer, and Cairnsmore-of-Fleet such a deep shade of blue.

Ma sighed deeply. Da would agree that they had much to be thankful for.